A VINTAGE CHRISTMAS

A COLLECTION OF CLASSIC STORIES AND POEMS

THOMAS NELSON
Since 1798

Editor's note: In order to preserve the authenticity of these works, many old, variant spellings of words have been maintained. We have made only minor adjustments to punctuation uses in order to improve readability.

ISBN: 978-1-4003-3785-9 (softcover)

Library of Congress Cataloging-in-Publication Data

Title: A vintage Christmas : a collection of classic stories and poems / Thomas Nelson.
Description: Nashville : Thomas Nelson, 2018.
Identifiers: LCCN 2018020633 | ISBN 9780785224136 (hardback)
Subjects: LCSH: Christmas stories, American. | Christmas stories, English. |
Christmas poetry, American. | Christmas poetry, English. |
Christmas
stories.
Classification: LCC PN6071.C6 V56 2018 | DDC 808.83/9334--dc23
LC record available at https://lccn.loc.gov/2018020633

Printed in the United States of America

23 24 25 26 27 LBC 5 4 3 2 1

CONTENTS

STORIES AND SKETCHES

CONTENTS

POEMS

STORIES AND SKETCHES

Louisa May Alcott

1832–1888

A CHRISTMAS DREAM, AND
HOW IT CAME TO BE TRUE

"I'm so tired of Christmas I wish there never would be another one!" exclaimed a discontented-looking little girl, as she sat idly watching her mother arrange a pile of gifts two days before they were to be given.

"Why, Effie, what a dreadful thing to say! You are as bad as old Scrooge; and I'm afraid something will happen to you, as it did to him, if you don't care for dear Christmas," answered mamma, almost dropping the silver horn she was filling with delicious candies.

"Who was Scrooge? What happened to him?" asked Effie, with a glimmer of interest in her listless face, as she picked out the sourest lemon-drop she could find; for nothing sweet suited her just then.

"He was one of Dickens's best people, and you can read the charming story some day. He hated Christmas until a strange dream showed him how dear and beautiful it was, and made a better man of him."

"I shall read it; for I like dreams, and have a great many curious ones myself. But they don't keep me from being tired of Christmas," said Effie, poking discontentedly among the sweeties for something worth eating.

"Why are you tired of what should be the happiest time of all the year?" asked mamma, anxiously.

"Perhaps I shouldn't be if I had something new. But it is always the same, and there isn't any more surprise about it. I always find heaps of goodies in my stocking. Don't like some of them, and soon get tired of those I do like. We always have a great dinner, and I eat too much, and feel ill next day. Then there is a Christmas tree somewhere, with a doll on top, or a stupid old Santa Claus, and children dancing and screaming over bonbons and toys that break, and shiny things that are of no use. Really, mamma, I've had so many Christmases all alike that I don't think I can bear another one." And Effie laid herself flat on the sofa, as if the mere idea was too much for her.

Her mother laughed at her despair, but was sorry to see her little girl so discontented, when she had everything to make her happy, and had known but ten Christmas days.

"Suppose we don't give you any presents at all,—how would that suit you?" asked mamma, anxious to please her spoiled child.

"I should like one large and splendid one, and one dear little one, to remember some very nice person by," said Effie, who was a fanciful little body, full of odd whims and notions, which her friends loved to gratify, regardless of time, trouble, or money; for she was the last of three little girls, and very dear to all the family.

"Well, my darling, I will see what I can do to please you, and not say a word until all is ready. If I could only get a new idea to start with!" And mamma went on tying up her pretty bundles with a thoughtful face, while Effie strolled to the window to watch the rain that kept her in-doors and made her dismal.

"Seems to me poor children have better times than rich ones. I can't go out, and there is a girl about my age splashing along, without any maid to fuss about rubbers and cloaks and umbrellas and colds. I wish I was a beggar-girl."

"Would you like to be hungry, cold, and ragged, to beg all day, and sleep on an ash-heap at night?" asked mamma, wondering what would come next.

"Cinderella did, and had a nice time in the end. This girl out here has a basket of scraps on her arm, and a big old shawl all round her, and doesn't seem to care a bit, though the water runs out of the toes of her boots. She goes paddling along, laughing at the rain, and eating a cold potato as if it tasted nicer than the chicken and ice-cream I had for dinner. Yes, I do think poor children are happier than rich ones."

"So do I, sometimes. At the Orphan Asylum today I saw two dozen merry little souls who have no parents, no home, and no hope of Christmas beyond a stick of candy or a cake. I wish you had been there to see how happy they were, playing with the old toys some richer children had sent them."

"You may give them all mine; I'm so tired of them I never want to see them again," said Effie, turning from the window to the pretty baby-house full of everything a child's heart could desire.

"I will, and let you begin again with something you

will not tire of, if I can only find it." And mamma knit her brows trying to discover some grand surprise for this child who didn't care for Christmas.

Nothing more was said then; and wandering off to the library, Effie found *A Christmas Carol*, and curling herself up in the sofa corner, read it all before tea. Some of it she did not understand; but she laughed and cried over many parts of the charming story, and felt better without knowing why.

All the evening she thought of poor Tiny Tim, Mrs. Cratchit with the pudding, and the stout old gentleman who danced so gayly that "his legs twinkled in the air." Presently bedtime arrived.

"Come, now, and toast your feet," said Effie's nurse, "while I do your pretty hair and tell stories."

"I'll have a fairy tale to-night, a very interesting one," commanded Effie, as she put on her blue silk wrapper and little fur-lined slippers to sit before the fire and have her long curls brushed.

So Nursey told her best tales; and when at last the child lay down under her lace curtains, her head was full of a curious jumble of Christmas elves, poor children, snow-storms, sugarplums, and surprises. So it is no wonder that she dreamed all night; and this was the dream, which she never quite forgot.

She found herself sitting on a stone, in the middle of a great field, all alone. The snow was falling fast, a bitter wind whistled by, and night was coming on. She felt hungry, cold, and tired, and did not know where to go nor what to do.

"I wanted to be a beggar-girl, and now I am one; but I don't like it, and wish somebody would come and take care of me. I don't know who I am, and I think I must be lost," thought Effie, with the curious interest one takes in one's self in dreams. But the more she thought about it, the more bewildered she felt. Faster fell the snow, colder blew the wind, darker grew the night; and poor Effie made up her mind that she was quite forgotten and left to freeze alone. The tears were chilled on her cheeks, her feet felt like icicles, and her heart died within her, so hungry, frightened, and forlorn was she. Laying her head on her knees, she gave herself up for lost, and sat there with the great flakes fast turning her to a little white mound, when suddenly the sound of music reached her, and starting up, she looked and listened with all her eyes and ears.

Far away a dim light shone, and a voice was heard

singing. She tried to run toward the welcome glimmer, but could not stir, and stood like a small statue of expectation while the light drew nearer, and the sweet words of the song grew clearer.

From our happy home
Through the world we roam
One week in all the year,
Making winter spring
With the joy we bring,
For Christmas-tide is here.

Now the eastern star
Shines from afar
To light the poorest home;
Hearts warmer grow,
Gifts freely flow,
For Christmas-tide has come.

Now gay trees rise
Before young eyes,
Abloom with tempting cheer;

Blithe voices sing,
And blithe bells ring,
For Christmas-tide is here.

Oh, happy chime,
Oh, blessed time,
That draws us all so near!
"Welcome, dear day,"
All creatures say,
For Christmas-tide is here.

A child's voice sang, a child's hand carried the little candle; and in the circle of soft light it shed, Effie saw a pretty child coming to her through the night and snow. A rosy, smiling creature, wrapped in white fur, with a wreath of green and scarlet holly on its shining hair, the magic candle in one hand, and the other outstretched as if to shower gifts and warmly press all other hands.

Effie forgot to speak as this bright vision came nearer, leaving no trace of footsteps in the snow, only lighting the way with its little candle, and filling the air with the music of its song.

"Dear child, you are lost, and I have come to find you," said the stranger, taking Effie's cold hands in his, with a smile like sunshine, while every holly berry glowed like a little fire.

"Do you know me?" asked Effie, feeling no fear, but a great gladness, at his coming.

"I know all children, and go to find them; for this is my holiday, and I gather them from all parts of the world to be merry with me once a year."

"Are you an angel?" asked Effie, looking for the wings.

"No; I am a Christmas spirit, and live with my mates in a pleasant place, getting ready for our holiday, when we are let out to roam about the world, helping make this a happy time for all who will let us in. Will you come and see how we work?"

"I will go anywhere with you. Don't leave me again," cried Effie, gladly.

"First I will make you comfortable. That is what we love to do. You are cold, and you shall be warm; hungry, and I will feed you; sorrowful, and I will make you gay."

With a wave of his candle all three miracles were wrought,—for the snow-flakes turned to a white fur cloak and hood on Effie's head and shoulders, a bowl of hot soup came sailing to her lips, and vanished when she had eagerly drunk the last drop; and suddenly the dismal field changed to a new world so full of wonders that all her troubles were forgotten in a minute. Bells were ringing so merrily that it was hard to keep from dancing. Green garlands hung on the walls, and every tree was a Christmas tree full of toys, and blazing with candles that never went out.

In one place many little spirits sewed like mad on warm clothes, turning off work faster than any sewing-machine ever invented, and great piles were made ready to be sent to poor people. Other busy creatures packed money into purses, and wrote checks which they sent flying away on the wind,—a lovely kind of snow-storm to fall into a world below full of poverty. Older and graver spirits were looking over piles of little books, in which the records of the past year were kept, telling how different people had spent it, and what sort of gifts they deserved. Some got peace, some disappointment, some remorse and sorrow, some great joy and hope. The rich had generous thoughts sent them; the poor, gratitude and contentment. Children had more love and duty to parents; and parents renewed patience, wisdom, and satisfaction for and in their children. No one was forgotten.

"Please tell me what splendid place this is?" asked Effie, as soon as she could collect her wits after the first look at all these astonishing things.

"This is the Christmas world; and here we work all the year round, never tired of getting ready for the happy day. See, these are the saints just setting off; for some have far to go, and the children must not be disappointed."

As he spoke the spirit pointed to four gates, out of which four great sleighs were just driving, laden with toys, while a jolly old Santa Claus sat in the middle of each, drawing on his mittens and tucking up his wraps for a long cold drive. "Why, I thought there was only one Santa Claus, and even he was a humbug," cried Effie, astonished at the sight.

"Never give up your faith in the sweet old stones, even after you come to see that they are only the pleasant shadow of a lovely truth."

Just then the sleighs went off with a great jingling of bells and pattering of reindeer hoofs, while all the spirits gave a cheer that was heard in the lower world, where people said, "Hear the stars sing."

"I never will say there isn't any Santa Claus again. Now, show me more."

"You will like to see this place, I think, and may learn something here perhaps."

The spirit smiled as he led the way to a little door, through which Effie peeped into a world of dolls. Baby-houses were in full blast, with dolls of all sorts going on like live people. Waxen ladies sat in their parlors elegantly dressed; black dolls cooked in the kitchens; nurses walked out with the bits of dollies; and the streets were full of tin soldiers marching, wooden horses prancing, express wag-ons rumbling, and little men hurrying to and fro. Shops were there, and tiny people buying legs of mutton, pounds of tea, mites of clothes, and everything dolls use or wear or want.

But presently she saw that in some ways the dolls improved upon the manners and customs of human beings, and she watched eagerly to learn why they did these things. A fine Paris doll driving in her carriage took up a black worsted Dinah who was hobbling along with a basket of clean clothes, and carried her to her journey's end, as if it were the proper thing to do. Another interesting china lady took off her comfortable red cloak and put it round a poor wooden creature done up in a paper shift, and so badly painted that its face would have sent some babies into fits.

"Seems to me I once knew a rich girl who didn't give her things to poor girls. I wish I could remember who she was, and tell her to be as kind as that china doll," said Effie, much touched at the sweet way the pretty creature wrapped up the poor fright, and then ran off in her little gray gown to buy a shiny fowl stuck on a wooden platter for her invalid mother's dinner.

"We recall these things to people's minds by dreams. I think the girl you speak of won't forget this one." And the spirit smiled, as if he enjoyed some joke which she did not see.

A little bell rang as she looked, and away scampered the children into the red-and-green school-house with the roof that lifted up, so one could see how nicely they sat at their desks with mites of books, or drew on the inch-square blackboards with crumbs of chalk.

"They know their lessons very well, and are as still as mice. We make a great racket at our school, and get bad marks every day. I shall tell the girls they had better mind what they do, or their dolls will be better scholars than they are," said Effie, much impressed, as she peeped in and saw no rod in the hand of the little mistress, who looked up and shook her head at the intruder, as if begging her to go away before the order of the school was disturbed.

Effie retired at once, but could not resist one look in at the window of a fine mansion, where the family were at dinner, the children behaved so well at table, and never grumbled a bit when their mamma said they could not have any more fruit. "Now, show me something else," she said, as they came again to the low door that led out of Doll-land. "You have seen how we prepare for Christmas; let me show you where we love best to send our good and happy gifts," answered the spirit, giving her his hand again.

"I know. I've seen ever so many," began Effie, thinking of her own Christmases.

"No, you have never seen what I will show you. Come away, and remember what you see to-night."

Like a flash that bright world vanished, and Effie found herself in a part of the city she had never seen before. It was far away from the gayer places, where every store was brilliant with lights and full of pretty things, and every house wore a festival air, while people hurried to and fro with merry greetings. It was down among the dingy streets where the poor lived, and where there was no making ready for Christmas.

Hungry women looked in at the shabby shops, longing to buy meat and bread, but empty pockets forbade. Tipsy men drank up their wages in the bar-rooms; and in many cold dark chambers little children huddled under the thin blankets, trying to forget their misery in sleep.

No nice dinners filled the air with savory smells, no gay trees dropped toys and bonbons into eager hands, no little stockings hung in rows beside the chimney-piece ready to be filled, no happy sounds of music, gay voices, and dancing feet were heard; and there were no signs of Christmas anywhere.

"Don't they have any in this place?" asked Effie, shivering, as she held fast the spirit's hand, following where he led her. "We come to bring it. Let me show you our best workers." And the spirit pointed to some sweet-faced men and women who came stealing into the poor houses, working such beautiful miracles that Effie could only stand and watch.

Some slipped money into the empty pockets, and sent the happy mothers to buy all the comforts they needed; others led the drunken men out of temptation, and took them home to find safer pleasures there. Fires were kindled on cold hearths, tables spread as if by magic, and warm clothes wrapped round shivering limbs. Flowers suddenly bloomed in the chambers of the sick; old people found themselves remembered; sad hearts were consoled by a tender word, and wicked ones softened by the story of Him who forgave all sin.

But the sweetest work was for the children; and Effie held her breath to watch these human fairies hang up and fill the little stockings without which a child's Christmas is not perfect, putting in things that once she would have thought very humble presents, but which now seemed beautiful and precious because these poor babies had nothing.

"That is so beautiful! I wish I could make merry Christmases as these good people do, and be loved and thanked as they are," said Effie, softly, as she watched the busy men and women do their work and steal away without thinking of any reward but their own satisfaction.

"You can if you will. I have shown you the way. Try it, and see how happy your own holiday will be hereafter."

As he spoke, the spirit seemed to put his arms about her, and vanished with a kiss.

"Oh, stay and show me more!" cried Effie, trying to hold him fast.

"Darling, wake up, and tell me why you are smiling in your sleep," said a voice in her ear; and opening her eyes, there was mamma bending over her, and morning sunshine streaming into the room.

"Are they all gone? Did you hear the bells? Wasn't it splendid?" she asked, rubbing her eyes, and looking about her for the pretty child who was so real and sweet.

"You have been dreaming at a great rate,—talking in your sleep, laughing, and clapping your hands as if you were cheering some one. Tell me what was so splendid," said mamma, smoothing the tumbled hair and lifting up the sleepy head. Then, while she was being dressed, Effie told her dream, and Nursey thought it very wonderful; but mamma smiled to see how curiously things the child had thought, read, heard, and seen through the day were mixed up in her sleep.

"The spirit said I could work lovely miracles if I tried; but I don't know how to begin, for I have no magic candle to make feasts appear, and light up groves of Christmas trees, as he did," said Effie, sorrowfully.

"Yes, you have. We will do it! we will do it!" And clapping her hands, mamma suddenly began to dance all over the room as if she had lost her wits.

"How? how? You must tell me, mamma," cried Effie, dancing after her, and ready to believe anything possible when she remembered the adventures of the past night.

"I've got it! I've got it!—the new idea. A splendid one, if I can only carry it out!" And mamma waltzed the little girl round till her curls flew wildly in the air, while Nursey laughed as if she would die.

"Tell me! tell me!" shrieked Effie. "No, no; it is a surprise,— a grand surprise for Christmas day!" sung mamma, evidently charmed with her happy thought. "Now, come to breakfast; for we must work like bees if we want to play spirits tomorrow. You and Nursey will go out shopping, and get heaps of things, while I arrange matters behind the scenes."

They were running downstairs as mamma spoke, and Effie called out breathlessly,—

"It won't be a surprise; for I know you are going to ask some poor children here, and have a tree or something. It won't be like my dream; for they had ever so many trees, and more children than we can find anywhere."

"There will be no tree, no party, no dinner, in this house at all, and no presents for you. Won't that be a surprise?" And mamma laughed at Effie's bewildered face.

"Do it. I shall like it, I think; and I won't ask any questions, so it will all burst upon me when the time comes," she said; and she ate her breakfast thoughtfully, for this really would be a new sort of Christmas.

All that morning Effie trotted after Nursey in and out of shops, buying dozens of barking dogs, woolly lambs, and squeaking birds; tiny tea-sets, gay picture-books, mittens and hoods, dolls and candy. Parcel after parcel was sent home; but when Effie returned she saw no trace of them, though she peeped everywhere. Nursey chuckled, but wouldn't give a hint, and went out again in the afternoon with a long list of more things to buy; while Effie wandered forlornly about the house, missing the usual merry stir that went before the Christmas dinner and the evening fun.

As for mamma, she was quite invisible all day, and came in at night so tired that she could only lie on the sofa to rest, smiling as if some very pleasant thought made her happy in spite of weariness.

"Is the surprise going on all right?" asked Effie, anxiously; for it seemed an immense time to wait till another evening came.

"Beautifully! better than I expected; for several of my good friends are helping, or I couldn't have done it as I wish. I know you will like it, dear, and long remember this new way of making Christmas merry."

Mamma gave her a very tender kiss, and Effie went to bed.

The next day was a very strange one; for when she woke there was no stocking to examine, no pile of gifts under her napkin, no one said "Merry Christmas!" to her, and the dinner was just as usual to her. Mamma vanished again, and Nursey kept wiping her eyes and saying: "The dear things! It's the prettiest idea I ever heard of. No one but your blessed ma could have done it."

"Do stop, Nursey, or I shall go crazy because I don't know the secret!" cried Effie, more than once; and she kept her eye on the clock, for at seven in the evening the surprise was to come off.

The longed-for hour arrived at last, and the child was too excited to ask questions when Nurse put on her cloak and hood, led her to the carriage, and they drove away, leaving their house the one dark and silent one in the row.

"I feel like the girls in the fairy tales who are led off to strange places and see fine things," said Effie, in a whisper, as they jingled through the gay streets.

"Ah, my deary, it is like a fairy tale, I do assure you, and you will see finer things than most children will tonight. Steady, now, and do just as I tell you, and don't say one word whatever you see," answered Nursey, quite quivering with excitement as she patted a large box in her lap, and nodded and laughed with twinkling eyes.

They drove into a dark yard, and Effie was led through a back door to a little room, where Nurse coolly proceeded to take off not only her cloak and hood, but her dress and shoes also. Effie stared and bit her lips, but kept still until out of the box came a little white fur coat and boots, a wreath of holly leaves and berries, and a candle with a frill of gold paper round it. A long "Oh!" escaped her then; and when she was dressed and saw herself in the glass, she started back, exclaiming, "Why, Nursey, I look like the spirit in my dream!"

"So you do; and that's the part you are to play, my pretty! Now whist, while I blind your eyes and put you in your place."

"Shall I be afraid?" whispered Effie, full of wonder; for as they went out she heard the sound of many voices, the tramp of many feet, and, in spite of the bandage, was sure a great light shone upon her when she stopped.

"You needn't be; I shall stand close by, and your ma will be there."

After the handkerchief was tied about her eyes, Nurse led Effie up some steps, and placed her on a high platform, where something like leaves touched her head, and the soft snap of lamps seemed to fill the air. Music began as soon as Nurse clapped her hands, the voices outside sounded nearer, and the tramp was evidently coming up the stairs.

"Now, my precious, look and see how you and your dear ma have made a merry Christmas for them that needed it!"

Off went the bandage; and for a minute Effie really did think she was asleep again, for she actually stood in "a grove of Christmas trees," all gay and shining as in her vision.

Twelve on a side, in two rows down the room, stood the little pines, each on its low table; and behind Effie a taller one rose to the roof, hung with wreaths of popcorn, apples, oranges, horns of candy, and cakes of all sorts, from sugary hearts to gingerbread Jumbos. On the smaller trees she saw many of her own discarded toys and those Nursey bought, as well as heaps that seemed to have rained down straight from that delightful Christmas country where she felt as if she was again.

"How splendid! Who is it for? What is that noise? Where is mamma?" cried Effie, pale with pleasure and surprise, as she stood looking down the brilliant little street from her high place.

Before Nurse could answer, the doors at the lower end flew open, and in marched twenty-four little blue-gowned orphan girls, singing sweetly, until amazement changed the song to cries of joy and wonder as the shining spectacle appeared. While they stood staring with round eyes at the wilderness of pretty things about them, mamma stepped up beside Effie, and holding her hand fast to give her courage, told the story of the dream in a few simple words, ending in this way:—

"So my little girl wanted to be a Christmas spirit too, and make this a happy day for those who had not as many pleasures and comforts as she has. She likes surprises, and we planned this for you all. She shall play the good fairy, and give each of you something from this tree, after which every one will find her own name on a small tree, and can go to enjoy it in her own way. March by, my dears, and let us fill your hands."

Nobody told them to do it, but all the hands were clapped heartily before a single child stirred; then one by one they came to look up wonderingly at the pretty giver of the feast as she leaned down to offer them great yellow oranges, red apples, bunches of grapes, bonbons, and cakes, till all were gone, and a double row of smiling faces turned toward her as the children filed back to their places in the orderly way they had been taught.

Then each was led to her own tree by the good ladies who had helped mamma with all their hearts; and the happy hubbub that arose would have satisfied even Santa Claus himself,—shrieks of joy, dances of delight, laughter and tears (for some tender little things could not bear so much pleasure at once, and sobbed with mouths full of candy and hands full of toys). How they ran to show one another the new treasures! how they peeped and tasted, pulled and pinched, until the air was full of queer noises, the floor covered with papers, and the little trees left bare of all but candles!

"I don't think heaven can be any gooder than this," sighed one small girl, as she looked about her in a blissful maze, holding her full apron with one hand, while she luxuriously carried sugar-plums to her mouth with the other.

"Is that a truly angel up there?" asked another, fascinated by the little white figure with the wreath on its shining hair, who in some mysterious way had been the cause of all this merry-making.

"I wish I dared to go and kiss her for this splendid party," said a lame child, leaning on her crutch, as she stood near the steps, wondering how it seemed to sit in a mother's lap, as Effie was doing, while she watched the happy scene before her. Effie heard her, and remembering Tiny Tim, ran down and put her arms about the pale child, kissing the wistful face, as she said sweetly, "You may; but mamma deserves the thanks. She did it all; I only dreamed about it."

Lame Katy felt as if "a truly angel" was embracing her,

and could only stammer out her thanks, while the other children ran to see the pretty spirit, and touch her soft dress, until she stood in a crowd of blue gowns laughing as they held up their gifts for her to see and admire.

Mamma leaned down and whispered one word to the older girls; and suddenly they all took hands to dance round Effie, singing as they skipped.

It was a pretty sight, and the ladies found it hard to break up the happy revel; but it was late for small people, and too much fun is a mistake. So the girls fell into line, and marched before Effie and mamma again, to say good-night with such grateful little faces that the eyes of those who looked grew dim with tears. Mamma kissed every one; and many a hungry childish heart felt as if the touch of those tender lips was their best gift. Effie shook so many small hands that her own tingled; and when Katy came she pressed a small doll into Effie's hand, whispering, "You didn't have a single present, and we had lots. Do keep that; it's the prettiest thing I got."

"I will," answered Effie, and held it fast until the last smiling face was gone, the surprise all over, and she safe in her own bed, too tired and happy for anything but sleep.

"Mamma, it was a beautiful surprise, and I thank you so much! I don't see how you did it; but I like it best of all the Christmases I ever had, and mean to make one every year. I had my splendid big present, and here is the dear little one to keep for love of poor Katy; so even that part of my wish came true."

And Effie fell asleep with a happy smile on her lips, her one humble gift still in her hand, and a new love for Christmas in her heart that never changed through a long life spent in doing good.

A COUNTRY CHRISTMAS

*"A handful of good life is worth
a bushel of learning."*

"Dear Emily,—I have a brilliant idea, and at once hasten to share it with you. Three weeks ago I came up here to the wilds of Vermont to visit my old aunt, also to get a little quiet and distance in which to survey certain new prospects which have opened before me, and to decide whether I will marry a millionnaire and become a queen of society, or remain 'the charming Miss Vaughan' and wait till the conquering hero comes.

"Aunt Plumy begs me to stay over Christmas, and I have

consented, as I always dread the formal dinner with which my guardian celebrates the day.

"My brilliant idea is this. I'm going to make it a real old-fashioned frolic, and won't you come and help me? You will enjoy it immensely I am sure, for Aunt is a character, Cousin Saul worth seeing, and Ruth a far prettier girl than any of the city rose-buds coming out this season. Bring Leonard Randal along with you to take notes for his new books; then it will be fresher and truer than the last, clever as it was.

"The air is delicious up here, society amusing, this old farmhouse full of treasures, and your bosom friend pining to embrace you. Just telegraph yes or no, and we will expect you on Tuesday.

"Ever yours,

"SOPHIE VAUGHAN."

"They will both come, for they are as tired of city life and as fond of change as I am," said the writer of the above, as she folded her letter and went to get it posted without delay.

Aunt Plumy was in the great kitchen making pies; a jolly old soul, with a face as ruddy as a winter apple, a cheery voice, and the kindest heart that ever beat under a gingham gown. Pretty Ruth was chopping the mince, and singing so gaily as she worked that the four-and-twenty immortal blackbirds could not have put more music into a pie than she did. Saul was piling wood into the big oven, and Sophie paused a moment on the threshold to look at him, for she always enjoyed the sight of this stalwart cousin, whom she likened to a Norse viking, with his fair hair and beard, keen blue eyes, and six feet of manly height, with shoulders that looked broad and strong enough to bear any burden.

His back was toward her, but he saw her first, and turned his flushed face to meet her, with the sudden lighting up it always showed when she approached.

"I've done it, Aunt; and now I want Saul to post the letter, so we can get a speedy answer."

"Just as soon as I can hitch up, cousin"; and Saul pitched in his last log, looking ready to put a girdle round the earth in less than forty minutes.

"Well, dear, I ain't the least mite of objection, as long as it pleases you. I guess we can stan' it ef your city folks can. I presume to say things will look kind of sing'lar to 'em, but I s'pose that's what they come for. Idle folks do dreadful queer things to amuse 'em"; and Aunt Plumy leaned on the rolling-pin to smile and nod with a shrewd twinkle of her eye, as if she enjoyed the prospect as much as Sophie did.

"I shall be afraid of 'em, but I'll try not to make you ashamed of me," said Ruth, who loved her charming cousin even more than she admired her.

"No fear of that, dear. They will be the awkward ones, and you must set them at ease by just being your simple selves, and treating them as if they were every-day people. Nell is very nice and jolly when she drops her city ways, as she must here. She will enter into the spirit of the fun at once, and I know you'll all like her. Mr. Randal is rather the worse for too much praise and petting, as successful people are apt to be, so a little plain talk and rough work will do him good. He is a true gentleman in spite of his airs and elegance, and he will take it all in good part, if you treat him like a man and not a lion."

"I'll see to him," said Saul, who had listened with great interest to the latter part of Sophie's speech, evidently suspecting a lover, and enjoying the idea of supplying him with a liberal amount of "plain talk and rough work."

"I'll keep 'em busy if that's what they need, for there

will be a sight to do, and we can't get help easy up here. Our darters don't hire out much. Work to home till they marry, and don't go gaddin' 'round gettin' their heads full of foolish notions, and forgettin' all the useful things their mothers taught 'em."

Aunt Plumy glanced at Ruth as she spoke, and a sudden color in the girl's cheeks proved that the words hit certain ambitious fancies of this pretty daughter of the house of Basset.

"They shall do their parts and not be a trouble; I'll see to that, for you certainly are the dearest aunt in the world to let me take possession of you and yours in this way," cried Sophie, embracing the old lady with warmth.

Saul wished the embrace could be returned by proxy, as his mother's hands were too floury to do more than hover affectionately round the delicate face that looked so fresh and young beside her wrinkled one. As it could not be done, he fled temptation and "hitched up" without delay.

The three women laid their heads together in his absence, and Sophie's plan grew apace, for Ruth longed to see a real novelist and a fine lady, and Aunt Plumy, having plans of her own to further, said "Yes, dear," to every suggestion.

Great was the arranging and adorning that went on that day in the old farmhouse, for Sophie wanted her friends to enjoy this taste of country pleasures, and knew just what additions would be indispensable to their comfort; what simple ornaments would be in keeping with the rustic stage on which she meant to play the part of prima donna.

Next day a telegram arrived accepting the invitation, for both the lady and the lion. They would arrive that afternoon, as little preparation was needed for this impromptu journey, the novelty of which was its chief charm to these *blasé* people.

Saul wanted to get out the double sleigh and span, for he prided himself on his horses, and a fall of snow came most opportunely to beautify the landscape and add a new pleasure to Christmas festivities.

But Sophie declared that the old yellow sleigh, with Punch, the farm-horse, must be used, as she wished everything to be in keeping; and Saul obeyed, thinking he had never seen anything prettier than his cousin when she appeared in his mother's old-fashioned camlet cloak and blue silk pumpkin hood. He looked remarkably well himself in his fur coat, with hair and beard brushed till they shone like spun gold, a fresh color in his cheek, and the sparkle of amusement in his eyes, while excitement gave his usually grave face the animation it needed to be handsome.

Away they jogged in the creaking old sleigh, leaving Ruth to make herself pretty, with a fluttering heart, and Aunt Plumy to dish up a late dinner fit to tempt the most fastidious appetite.

"She has not come for us, and there is not even a stage to take us up. There must be some mistake," said Emily Herrick, as she looked about the shabby little station where they were set down.

"That is the never-to-be-forgotten face of our fair friend, but the bonnet of her grandmother, if my eyes do not deceive me," answered Randal, turning to survey the couple approaching in the rear.

"Sophie Vaughan, what do you mean by making such a guy of yourself?" exclaimed Emily, as she kissed the smiling face in the hood and stared at the quaint cloak.

"I'm dressed for my part, and I intend to keep it up. This is our host, my cousin, Saul Basset. Come to the sleigh at once, he will see to your luggage," said Sophie, painfully conscious of the antiquity of her array as her eyes rested on

Emily's pretty hat and mantle, and the masculine elegance of Randal's wraps.

They were hardly tucked in when Saul appeared with a valise in one hand and a large trunk on his shoulder, swinging both on to a wood-sled that stood near by as easily as if they had been hand-bags.

"That is your hero, is it? Well, he looks it, calm and comely, taciturn and tall," said Emily, in a tone of approbation.

"He should have been named Samson or Goliath; though I believe it was the small man who slung things about and turned out the hero in the end," added Randal, surveying the performance with interest and a touch of envy, for much pen work had made his own hands as delicate as a woman's.

"Saul doesn't live in a glass house, so stones won't hurt him. Remember sarcasm is forbidden and sincerity the order of the day. You are country folks now, and it will do you good to try their simple, honest ways for a few days."

Sophie had no time to say more, for Saul came up and drove off with the brief remark that the baggage would "be along right away."

Being hungry, cold and tired, the guests were rather

silent during the short drive, but Aunt Plumy's hospitable welcome, and the savory fumes of the dinner awaiting them, thawed the ice and won their hearts at once.

"Isn't it nice? Aren't you glad you came?" asked Sophie, as she led her friends into the parlor, which she had redeemed from its primness by putting bright chintz curtains to the windows, hemlock boughs over the old portraits, a china bowl of flowers on the table, and a splendid fire on the wide hearth.

"It is perfectly jolly, and this is the way I begin to enjoy myself," answered Emily, sitting down upon the home-made rug, whose red flannel roses bloomed in a blue list basket.

"If I may add a little smoke to your glorious fire, it will be quite perfect. Won't Samson join me?" asked Randal, waiting for permission, cigar-case in hand.

"He has no small vices, but you may indulge yours," answered Sophie, from the depths of a grandmotherly chair.

Emily glanced up at her friend as if she caught a new tone in her voice, then turned to the fire again with a wise little nod, as if confiding some secret to the reflection of herself in the bright brass andiron.

"His Delilah does not take this form. I wait with interest to discover if he has one. What a daisy the sister is. Does she ever speak?" asked Randal, trying to lounge on the haircloth sofa, where he was slipping uncomfortably about.

"Oh yes, and sings like a bird. You shall hear her when she gets over her shyness. But no trifling, mind you, for it is a jealously guarded daisy and not to be picked by any idle hand," said Sophie warningly, as she recalled Ruth's blushes and Randal's compliments at dinner.

"I should expect to be annihilated by the big brother if I attempted any but the 'sincerest' admiration and respect. Have no fears on that score, but tell us what is to follow this superb dinner. An apple bee, spinning match, husking party, or primitive pastime of some sort, I have no doubt."

"As you are new to our ways I am going to let you rest this evening. We will sit about the fire and tell stories. Aunt is a master hand at that, and Saul has reminiscences of the war that are well worth hearing if we can only get him to tell them."

"Ah, he was there, was he?"

"Yes, all through it, and is Major Basset, though he likes his plain name best. He fought splendidly and had several wounds, though only a mere boy when he earned his scars and bars. I'm very proud of him for that," and Sophie looked so as she glanced at the photograph of a stripling in uniform set in the place of honor on the high mantel-piece.

"We must stir him up and hear these martial memories. I want some new incidents, and shall book all I can get, if I may."

Here Randal was interrupted by Saul himself, who came in with an armful of wood for the fire.

"Anything more I can do for you, cousin?" he asked, surveying the scene with a rather wistful look.

"Only come and sit with us and talk over war times with Mr. Randal."

"When I've foddered the cattle and done my chores I'd be pleased to. What regiment were you in?" asked Saul, looking down from his lofty height upon the slender gentleman, who answered briefly,—

"In none. I was abroad at the time."

"Sick?"

"No, busy with a novel."

"Took four years to write it?"

"I was obliged to travel and study before I could finish

it. These things take more time to work up than outsiders would believe."

"Seems to me our war was a finer story than any you could find in Europe, and the best way to study it would be to fight it out. If you want heroes and heroines you'd have found plenty of 'em there."

"I have no doubt of it, and shall be glad to atone for my seeming neglect of them by hearing about your own exploits, Major."

Randal hoped to turn the conversation gracefully, but Saul was not to be caught, and left the room, saying, with a gleam of fun in his eye,—

"I can't stop now; heroes can wait, pigs can't."

The girls laughed at this sudden descent from the sublime to the ridiculous, and Randal joined them, feeling his condescension had not been unobserved.

As if drawn by the merry sound Aunt Plumy appeared, and being established in the rocking-chair fell to talking as easily as if she had known her guests for years.

"Laugh away, young folks, that's better for digestion than any of the messes people use. Are you troubled with dyspepsy, dear? You didn't seem to take your vittles very hearty, so I mistrusted you was delicate," she said, looking at Emily, whose pale cheeks and weary eyes told the story of late hours and a gay life.

"I haven't eaten so much for years, I assure you, Mrs. Basset; but it was impossible to taste all your good things. I am not dyspeptic, thank you, but a little seedy and tired, for I've been working rather hard lately."

"Be you a teacher? or have you a 'perfessun,' as they call a trade nowadays?" asked the old lady in a tone of kindly interest, which prevented a laugh at the idea of Emily's being anything but a beauty and a belle. The others kept their countenances with difficulty, and she answered demurely,—

"I have no trade as yet, but I dare say I should be happier if I had."

"Not a doubt on't, my dear."

"What would you recommend, ma'am?"

"I should say dressmakin' was rather in your line, ain't it? Your clothes is dreadful tasty, and do you credit if you made 'em yourself," and Aunt Plumy surveyed with feminine interest the simple elegance of the travelling dress which was the masterpiece of a French modiste.

"No, ma'am, I don't make my own things, I'm too lazy.

It takes so much time and trouble to select them that I have only strength left to wear them."

"Housekeepin' used to be the favorite perfessun in my day. It ain't fashionable now, but it needs a sight of trainin' to be perfect in all that's required, and I've an idee it would be a sight healthier and usefuller than the paintin' and music and fancy work young women do nowadays."

"But every one wants some beauty in their lives, and each one has a different sphere to fill, if one can only find it."

"'Pears to me there's no call for so much art when nater is full of beauty for them that can see and love it. As for 'spears' and so on, I've a notion if each of us did up our own little chores smart and thorough we needn't go wanderin' round to set the world to rights. That's the Lord's job, and I presume to say He can do it without any advice of ourn."

Something in the homely but true words seemed to rebuke the three listeners for wasted lives, and for a moment there was no sound but the crackle of the fire, the brisk click of the old lady's knitting needles, and Ruth's voice singing overhead as she made ready to join the party below.

"To judge by that sweet sound you have done one of your 'chores' very beautifully, Mrs. Basset, and in spite of the follies of our day, succeeded in keeping one girl healthy, happy and unspoiled," said Emily, looking up into the peaceful old face with her own lovely one full of respect and envy.

"I do hope so, for she's my ewe lamb, the last of four dear little girls; all the rest are in the burying ground 'side of father. I don't expect to keep her long, and don't ought to regret when I lose her, for Saul is the best of sons; but daughters is more to mothers somehow, and I always yearn over girls that is left without a broodin' wing to keep 'em safe and warm in this world of tribulation."

Aunt Plumy laid her hand on Sophie's head as she spoke, with such a motherly look that both girls drew nearer, and Randal resolved to put her in a book without delay.

Presently Saul returned with little Ruth hanging on his arm and shyly nestling near him as he took the three-cornered leathern chair in the chimney nook, while she sat on a stool close by.

"Now the circle is complete and the picture perfect. Don't light the lamps yet, please, but talk away and let me make a mental study of you. I seldom find so charming a scene to paint," said Randal, beginning to enjoy himself immensely, with a true artist's taste for novelty and effect.

"Tell us about your book, for we have been reading it as it comes out in the magazine, and are much exercised about how it's going to end," began Saul, gallantly throwing himself into the breach, for a momentary embarrassment fell upon the women at the idea of sitting for their portraits before they were ready.

"Do you really read my poor serial up here, and do me the honor to like it?" asked the novelist, both flattered and amused, for his work was of the aesthetic sort, microscopic studies of character, and careful pictures of modern life.

"Sakes alive, why shouldn't we," cried Aunt Plumy. "We have some eddication, though we ain't very genteel. We've got a town libry, kep up by the women mostly, with fairs and tea parties and so on. We have all the magazines reg'lar, and Saul reads out the pieces while Ruth sews and I knit, my eyes bein' poor. Our winter is long and evenins would be kinder lonesome if we didn't have novils and newspapers to cheer 'em up."

"I am very glad I can help to beguile them for you. Now tell me what you honestly think of my work? Criticism is always valuable, and I should really like yours, Mrs. Basset," said Randal, wondering what the good woman would make of the delicate analysis and worldly wisdom on which he prided himself.

Short work, as Aunt Plumy soon showed him, for she rather enjoyed freeing her mind at all times, and decidedly resented the insinuation that country folk could not appreciate light literature as well as city people.

"I ain't no great of a jedge about anything but nat'ralness of books, and it really does seem as if some of your men and women was dreadful uncomfortable creaters. 'Pears to me it ain't wise to be always pickin' ourselves to pieces and pryin' into things that ought to come gradual by way of experience and the visitations of Providence. Flowers won't blow worth a cent ef you pull 'em open. Better wait and see what they can do alone. I do relish the smart sayins, the odd ways of furrin parts, and the sarcastic slaps at folkses weak spots. But, massy knows, we can't live on spice-cake and Charlotte Ruche, and I do feel as if books was more sustainin' ef they was full of every-day people and things, like good bread and butter. Them that goes to the heart and ain't soon forgotten is the kind I hanker for. Mis Terry's books now, and Mis Stowe's, and Dickens's Christmas pieces,—them is real sweet and cheerin', to my mind."

As the blunt old lady paused it was evident she had produced a sensation, for Saul smiled at the fire, Ruth looked dismayed at this assault upon one of her idols, and the young ladies were both astonished and amused at the keenness of the new critic who dared express what they had often felt. Randal, however, was quite composed and laughed good-naturedly, though secretly feeling as if a pail of cold water had been poured over him.

"Many thanks, madam; you have discovered my weak point with surprising accuracy. But you see I cannot help 'picking folks to pieces,' as you have expressed it; that is my gift, and it has its attractions, as the sale of my books will testify. People like the 'spice-bread,' and as that is the only sort my oven will bake, I must keep on in order to make my living."

"So rumsellers say, but it ain't a good trade to foller, and I'd chop wood 'fore I'd earn my livin' harmin' my feller man. 'Pears to me I'd let my oven cool a spell, and hunt up some homely, happy folks to write about; folks that don't borrer trouble and go lookin' for holes in their neighbors' coats, but take their lives brave and cheerful; and rememberin' we are all human, have pity on the weak, and try to be as full of mercy, patience and lovin' kindness as Him who made us. That sort of a book would do a heap of good; be real warmin' and strengthenin', and make them that read it love the man that wrote it, and remember him when he was dead and gone."

"I wish I could!" and Randal meant what he said, for he was as tired of his own style, as a watch-maker might be of the magnifying glass through which he strains his eyes all day. He knew that the heart was left out of his work, and that both mind and soul were growing morbid with dwelling on the faulty, absurd and metaphysical phases of life and character. He often threw down his pen and vowed he would write no more; but he loved ease and the books brought money readily; he was accustomed to the stimulant of praise and missed it as the toper misses his wine, so that which had once been a pleasure to himself and others was fast becoming a burden and a disappointment.

The brief pause which followed his involuntary betrayal of discontent was broken by Ruth, who exclaimed, with a girlish enthusiasm that overpowered girlish bashfulness,—

"*I* think all the novels are splendid! I hope you will write hundreds more, and I shall live to read 'em."

"Bravo, my gentle champion! I promise that I will write one more at least, and have a heroine in it whom your mother will both admire and love," answered Randal, surprised to find how grateful he was for the girl's approval, and how rapidly his trained fancy began to paint the background on which he hoped to copy this fresh, human daisy.

Abashed by her involuntary outburst, Ruth tried to efface herself behind Saul's broad shoulder, and he brought the conversation back to its starting-point by saying in a tone of the most sincere interest,—

"Speaking of the serial, I am very anxious to know how your hero comes out. He is a fine fellow, and I can't decide whether he is going to spoil his life marrying that silly woman, or do something grand and generous, and not be made a fool of."

"Upon my soul, I don't know myself. It is very hard to find new finales. Can't you suggest something, Major? then I shall not be obliged to leave my story without an end, as people complain I am rather fond of doing."

"Well, no, I don't think I've anything to offer. Seems to me it isn't the sensational exploits that show the hero best, but some great sacrifice quietly made by a common sort of man who is noble without knowing it. I saw a good many such during the war, and often wish I could write them down, for it is surprising how much courage, goodness and real piety is stowed away in common folks ready to show when the right time comes."

"Tell us one of them, and I'll bless you for a hint. No one knows the anguish of an author's spirit when he can't ring down the curtain on an effective tableau," said Randal, with a glance at his friends to ask their aid in eliciting an anecdote or reminiscence.

"Tell about the splendid fellow who held the bridge, like Horatius, till help came up. That was a thrilling story, I assure you," answered Sophie, with an inviting smile.

But Saul would not be his own hero, and said briefly:

"Any man can be brave when the battle-fever is on him, and it only takes a little physical courage to dash ahead." He paused a moment, with his eyes on the snowy landscape without, where twilight was deepening; then, as if constrained by the memory that winter scene evoked, he slowly continued,—

"One of the bravest things I ever knew was done by a poor fellow who has been a hero to me ever since, though I only met him that night. It was after one of the big battles of that last winter, and I was knocked over with a broken leg and two or three bullets here and there. Night was coming on, snow falling, and a sharp wind blew over the field where a lot of us lay, dead and alive, waiting for the ambulance to come and pick us up. There was skirmishing going on not far off, and our prospects were rather poor between frost and fire. I was calculating how I'd manage, when I found two poor chaps close by who were worse off, so I braced up and did what I could for them. One had an arm blown away, and kept up a dreadful groaning. The other was shot bad, and bleeding to death for want of help, but never complained. He was nearest, and I liked his pluck, for he spoke cheerful and made me ashamed to growl. Such times make dreadful brutes of men if they haven't something to hold on to, and all three of us were most wild with pain and cold and hunger, for we'd fought all day fasting, when we heard a rumble in the road below, and saw lanterns bobbing round. That meant life to us, and we all tried to holler; two of us were pretty faint, but I managed a good yell, and they heard it.

"'Room for one more. Hard luck, old boys, but we are

full and must save the worst wounded first. Take a drink, and hold on till we come back,' says one of them with the stretcher.

"'Here's the one to go,' I says, pointin' out my man, for I saw by the light that he was hard hit.

"'No, that one. He's got more chances than I, or this one; he's young and got a mother; I'll wait,' said the good feller, touchin' my arm, for he'd heard me mutterin' to myself about this dear old lady. We always want mother when we are down, you know."

Saul's eyes turned to the beloved face with a glance of tenderest affection, and Aunt Plumy answered with a dismal groan at the recollection of his need that night, and her absence.

"Well, to be short, the groaning chap was taken, and my man left. I was mad, but there was no time for talk, and the selfish one went off and left that poor feller to run his one chance. I had my rifle, and guessed I could hobble up to use it if need be; so we settled back to wait without much hope of help, everything being in a muddle. And wait we did till morning, for that ambulance did not come back till next day, when most of us were past needing it.

"I'll never forget that night. I dream it all over again as plain as if it was real. Snow, cold, darkness, hunger, thirst, pain, and all round us cries and cursing growing less and less, till at last only the wind went moaning over that meadow. It was awful! so lonesome, helpless, and seemingly God-forsaken. Hour after hour we lay there side by side under one coat, waiting to be saved or die, for the wind grew strong and we grew weak."

Saul drew a long breath, and held his hands to the fire as if he felt again the sharp suffering of that night.

"And the man?" asked Emily, softly, as if reluctant to break the silence.

"He *was* a man! In times like that men talk like brothers and show what they are. Lying there, slowly freezing, Joe Cummings told me about his wife and babies, his old folks waiting for him, all depending on him, yet all ready to give him up when he was needed. A plain man, but honest and true, and loving as a woman; I soon saw that as he went on talking, half to me and half to himself, for sometimes he wandered a little toward the end. I've read books, heard sermons, and seen good folks, but nothing ever came so close or did me so much good as seeing this man die. He had one chance and gave it cheerfully. He longed for those he loved, and let 'em go with a good-by they couldn't hear. He suffered all the pains we most shrink from without a murmur, and kept my heart warm while his own was growing cold. It's no use trying to tell that part of it; but I heard prayers that night that meant something, and I saw how faith could hold a soul up when everything was gone but God."

Saul stopped there with a sudden huskiness in his deep voice, and when he went on it was in the tone of one who speaks of a dear friend.

"Joe grew still by and by, and I thought he was asleep, for I felt his breath when I tucked him up, and his hand held on to mine. The cold sort of numbed me, and I dropped off, too weak and stupid to think or feel. I never should have waked up if it hadn't been for Joe. When I came to, it was morning, and I thought I was dead, for all I could see was that great field of white mounds, like graves, and a splendid sky above. Then I looked for Joe, remembering; but he had put my coat back over me, and lay stiff and still under the snow that covered him like a shroud, all except his face. A bit of my cape had blown over it, and when I took it off and the sun shone on his dead face, I declare to you it was so full of heavenly peace I felt as if that common man had been glorified by God's light, and rewarded by God's 'Well done.' That's all."

No one spoke for a moment, while the women wiped their eyes, and Saul dropped his as if to hide something softer than tears.

"It was very noble, very touching. And you? how did you get off at last?" asked Randal, with real admiration and respect in his usually languid face.

"Crawled off," answered Saul, relapsing into his former brevity of speech.

"Why not before, and save yourself all that misery?"

"Couldn't leave Joe."

"Ah, I see; there were two heroes that night."

"Dozens, I've no doubt. Those were times that made heroes of men, and women, too."

"Tell us more," begged Emily, looking up with an expression none of her admirers ever brought to her face by their softest compliments or wiliest gossip.

"I've done my part. It's Mr. Randal's turn now"; and Saul drew himself out of the ruddy circle of firelight, as if ashamed of the prominent part he was playing.

Sophie and her friend had often heard Randal talk, for he was an accomplished *raconteur,* but that night he exerted himself, and was unusually brilliant and entertaining, as if upon his mettle. The Bassets were charmed. They sat late and were very merry, for Aunt Plumy got up a little supper for them, and her cider was as exhilarating as champagne. When they parted for the night and Sophie kissed her aunt, Emily did the same, saying heartily,—

"It seems as if I'd known you all my life, and this is certainly the most enchanting old place that ever was."

"Glad you like it, dear. But it ain't all fun, as you'll find out to-morrow when you go to work, for Sophie says you must," answered Mrs. Basset, as her guests trooped away, rashly promising to like everything.

They found it difficult to keep their word when they were called at half past six next morning. Their rooms were warm, however, and they managed to scramble down in time for breakfast, guided by the fragrance of coffee and Aunt Plumy's shrill voice singing the good old hymn—

"Lord, in the morning Thou shalt hear
My voice ascending high."

An open fire blazed on the hearth, for the cooking was

done in the lean-to, and the spacious, sunny kitchen was kept in all its old-fashioned perfection, with the wooden settle in a warm nook, the tall clock behind the door, copper and pewter utensils shining on the dresser, old china in the corner closet and a little spinning wheel rescued from the garret by Sophie to adorn the deep window, full of scarlet geraniums, Christmas roses, and white chrysanthemums.

The young lady, in a checked apron and mob-cap, greeted her friends with a dish of buckwheats in one hand, and a pair of cheeks that proved she had been learning to fry these delectable cakes.

"You do 'keep it up' in earnest, upon my word; and very becoming it is, dear. But won't you ruin your complexion and roughen your hands if you do so much of this new fancy-work?" asked Emily, much amazed at this novel freak.

"I like it, and really believe I've found my proper sphere at last. Domestic life seems so pleasant to me that I feel as if I'd better keep it up for the rest of my life," answered Sophie, making a pretty picture of herself as she cut great slices of brown bread, with the early sunshine touching her happy face.

"The charming Miss Vaughan in the role of a farmer's

wife. I find it difficult to imagine, and shrink from the thought of the wide-spread dismay such a fate will produce among her adorers," added Randal, as he basked in the glow of the hospitable fire.

"She might do worse; but come to breakfast and do honor to my handiwork," said Sophie, thinking of her worn-out millionnaire, and rather nettled by the satiric smile on Randal's lips.

"What an appetite early rising gives one. I feel equal to almost anything, so let me help wash cups," said Emily, with unusual energy, when the hearty meal was over and Sophie began to pick up the dishes as if it was her usual work.

Ruth went to the window to water the flowers, and Randal followed to make himself agreeable, remembering her defence of him last night. He was used to admiration from feminine eyes, and flattery from soft lips, but found something new and charming in the innocent delight which showed itself at his approach in blushes more eloquent than words, and shy glances from eyes full of hero-worship.

"I hope you are going to spare me a posy for to-morrow night, since I can be fine in no other way to do honor to the dance Miss Sophie proposes for us," he said, leaning in the bay window to look down on the little girl, with the devoted air he usually wore for pretty women.

"Anything you like! I should be so glad to have you wear my flowers. There will be enough for all, and I've nothing else to give to people who have made me as happy as cousin Sophie and you," answered Ruth, half drowning her great calla as she spoke with grateful warmth.

"You must make her happy by accepting the invitation to go home with her which I heard given last night. A peep at the world would do you good, and be a pleasant change, I think."

"Oh, very pleasant! but would it do me good?" and Ruth looked up with sudden seriousness in her blue eyes, as a child questions an elder, eager, yet wistful.

"Why not?" asked Randal, wondering at the hesitation.

"I might grow discontented with things here if I saw splendid houses and fine people. I am very happy now, and it would break my heart to lose that happiness, or ever learn to be ashamed of home."

"But don't you long for more pleasure, new scenes and other friends than these?" asked the man, touched by the little creature's loyalty to the things she knew and loved.

"Very often, but mother says when I'm ready they will come, so I wait and try not to be impatient." But Ruth's eyes looked out over the green leaves as if the longing was very strong within her to see more of the unknown world lying beyond the mountains that hemmed her in.

"It is natural for birds to hop out of the nest, so I shall expect to see you over there before long, and ask you how you enjoy your first flight," said Randal, in a paternal tone that had a curious effect on Ruth.

To his surprise, she laughed, then blushed like one of her own roses, and answered with a demure dignity that was very pretty to see.

"I intend to hop soon, but it won't be a very long flight or very far from mother. She can't spare me, and nobody in the world can fill her place to me."

Bless the child, does she think I'm going to make love to her, thought Randal, much amused, but quite mistaken. Wiser women had thought so when he assumed the caressing air with which he beguiled them into the little revelations of character he liked to use, as the south wind makes flowers open their hearts to give up their odor, then leaves them to carry it elsewhere, the more welcome for the stolen sweetness.

"Perhaps you are right. The maternal wing is a safe shelter for confiding little souls like you, Miss Ruth. You will be as comfortable here as your flowers in this sunny window," he said, carelessly pinching geranium leaves, and ruffling the roses till the pink petals of the largest fluttered to the floor.

As if she instinctively felt and resented something in the man which his act symbolized, the girl answered quietly, as she went on with her work, "Yes, if the frost does not touch me, or careless people spoil me too soon."

Before Randal could reply Aunt Plumy approached like a maternal hen who sees her chicken in danger.

"Saul is goin' to haul wood after he's done his chores, mebbe you'd like to go along? The view is good, the roads well broke, and the day uncommon fine."

"Thanks; it will be delightful, I dare say," politely responded the lion, with a secret shudder at the idea of a rural promenade at 8 a.m. in the winter.

"Come on, then; we'll feed the stock, and then I'll show you how to yoke oxen," said Saul, with a twinkle in his eye as he led the way, when his new aide had muffled himself up as if for a polar voyage.

"Now, that's too bad of Saul! He did it on purpose, just

to please you, Sophie," cried Ruth presently, and the girls ran to the window to behold Randal bravely following his host with a pail of pigs' food in each hand, and an expression of resigned disgust upon his aristocratic face.

"To what base uses may we come," quoted Emily, as they all nodded and smiled upon the victim as he looked back from the barn-yard, where he was clamorously welcomed by his new charges.

"It is rather a shock at first, but it will do him good, and Saul won't be too hard upon him, I'm sure," said Sophie, going back to her work, while Ruth turned her best buds to the sun that they might be ready for a peace-offering to-morrow.

There was a merry clatter in the big kitchen for an hour; then Aunt Plumy and her daughter shut themselves up in the pantry to perform some culinary rites, and the young ladies went to inspect certain antique costumes laid forth in Sophie's room.

"You see, Em, I thought it would be appropriate to the house and season to have an old-fashioned dance. Aunt has quantities of ancient finery stowed away, for great-grandfather Basset was a fine old gentleman and his family lived in state. Take your choice of the crimson, blue or silver-gray damask. Ruth is to wear the worked muslin and quilted white satin skirt, with that coquettish hat."

"Being dark, I'll take the red and trim it up with this fine lace. You must wear the blue and primrose, with the distracting high-heeled shoes. Have you any suits for the men?" asked Emily, throwing herself at once into the all-absorbing matter of costume.

"A claret velvet coat and vest, silk stockings, cocked hat and snuff-box for Randal. Nothing large enough for Saul, so he must wear his uniform. Won't Aunt Plumy be superb in this plum-colored satin and immense cap?"

A delightful morning was spent in adapting the faded finery of the past to the blooming beauty of the present, and time and tongues flew till the toot of a horn called them down to dinner.

The girls were amazed to see Randal come whistling up the road with his trousers tucked into his boots, blue mittens on his hands, and an unusual amount of energy in his whole figure, as he drove the oxen, while Saul laughed at his vain attempts to guide the bewildered beasts.

"It's immense! The view from the hill is well worth

seeing, for the snow glorifies the landscape and reminds one of Switzerland. I'm going to make a sketch of it this afternoon; better come and enjoy the delicious freshness, young ladies."

Randal was eating with such an appetite that he did not see the glances the girls exchanged as they promised to go.

"Bring home some more winter-green, I want things to be real nice, and we haven't enough for the kitchen," said Ruth, dimpling with girlish delight as she imagined herself dancing under the green garlands in her grandmother's wedding gown.

It was very lovely on the hill, for far as the eye could reach lay the wintry landscape sparkling with the brief beauty of sunshine on virgin snow. Pines sighed overhead, hardy birds flitted to and fro, and in all the trodden spots rose the little spires of evergreen ready for its Christmas duty. Deeper in the wood sounded the measured ring of axes, the crash of falling trees, while the red shirts of the men added color to the scene, and a fresh wind brought the aromatic breath of newly cloven hemlock and pine.

"How beautiful it is! I never knew before what winter woods were like. Did you, Sophie?" asked Emily, sitting on a stump to enjoy the novel pleasure at her ease.

"I've found out lately; Saul lets me come as often as I like, and this fine air seems to make a new creature of me," answered Sophie, looking about her with sparkling eyes, as if this was a kingdom where she reigned supreme.

"Something is making a new creature of you, that is very evident. I haven't yet discovered whether it is the air or some magic herb among that green stuff you are gathering so diligently"; and Emily laughed to see the color deepen beautifully in her friend's half-averted face.

"Scarlet is the only wear just now, I find. If we are lost like babes in the woods there are plenty of redbreasts to cover us with leaves," and Randal joined Emily's laugh, with a glance at Saul, who had just pulled his coat off.

"You wanted to see this tree go down, so stand from under and I'll show you how it's done," said the farmer, taking up his axe, not unwilling to gratify his guests and display his manly accomplishments at the same time.

It was a fine sight, the stalwart man swinging his axe with magnificent strength and skill, each blow sending a thrill through the stately tree, till its heart was reached and it tottered to its fall. Never pausing for breath Saul shook his yellow mane out of his eyes, and hewed away, while the drops stood on his forehead and his arm ached, as bent on distinguishing himself as if he had been a knight tilting against his rival for his lady's favor.

"I don't know which to admire most, the man or his muscle. One doesn't often see such vigor, size and comeliness in these degenerate days," said Randal, mentally booking the fine figure in the red shirt.

"I think we have discovered a rough diamond. I only wonder if Sophie is going to try and polish it," answered Emily, glancing at her friend, who stood a little apart, watching the rise and fall of the axe as intently as if her fate depended on it.

Down rushed the tree at last, and, leaving them to examine a crow's nest in its branches, Saul went off to his men, as if he found the praises of his prowess rather too much for him.

Randal fell to sketching, the girls to their garland-making, and for a little while the sunny woodland nook was full of lively chat and pleasant laughter, for the air exhilarated them all like wine. Suddenly a man came running from the wood, pale and anxious, saying, as he hastened by for help, "Blasted tree fell on him! Bleed to death before the doctor comes!"

"Who? who?" cried the startled trio.

But the man ran on, with some breathless reply, in which only a name was audible—"Basset."

"The deuce it is!" and Randal dropped his pencil, while the girls sprang up in dismay. Then, with one impulse, they hastened to the distant group, half visible behind the fallen trees and corded wood.

Sophie was there first, and forcing her way through the little crowd of men, saw a red-shirted figure on the ground, crushed and bleeding, and threw herself down beside it with a cry that pierced the hearts of those who heard it.

In the act she saw it was not Saul, and covered her bewildered face as if to hide its joy. A strong arm lifted her, and the familiar voice said cheeringly,—

"I'm all right, dear. Poor Bruce is hurt, but we've sent for help. Better go right home and forget all about it."

"Yes, I will, if I can do nothing"; and Sophie meekly returned to her friends who stood outside the circle over which Saul's head towered, assuring them of his safety.

Hoping they had not seen her agitation, she led Emily away, leaving Randal to give what aid he could and bring them news of the poor wood-chopper's state.

Aunt Plumy produced the "camphire" the moment she

saw Sophie's pale face, and made her lie down, while the brave old lady trudged briskly off with bandages and brandy to the scene of action. On her return she brought comfortable news of the man, so the little flurry blew over and was forgotten by all but Sophie, who remained pale and quiet all the evening, tying evergreen as if her life depended on it.

"A good night's sleep will set her up. She ain't used to such things, dear child, and needs cossetin'," said Aunt Plumy, purring over her until she was in her bed, with a hot stone at her feet and a bowl of herb tea to quiet her nerves.

An hour later when Emily went up, she peeped in to see if Sophie was sleeping nicely, and was surprised to find the invalid wrapped in a dressing-gown writing busily.

"Last will and testament, or sudden inspiration, dear? How are you? faint or feverish, delirious or in the dumps! Saul looks so anxious, and Mrs. Basset hushes us all up so, I came to bed, leaving Randal to entertain Ruth."

As she spoke Emily saw the papers disappear in a portfolio, and Sophie rose with a yawn.

"I was writing letters, but I'm sleepy now. Quite over my foolish fright, thank you. Go and get your beauty sleep that you may dazzle the natives to-morrow."

"So glad, good night"; and Emily went away, saying to herself, "Something is going on, and I must find out what it is before I leave. Sophie can't blind *me*."

But Sophie did all the next day, being delightfully gay at the dinner, and devoting herself to the young minister who was invited to meet the distinguished novelist, and evidently being afraid of him, gladly basked in the smiles of his charming neighbor. A dashing sleigh-ride occupied the afternoon, and then great was the fun and excitement over the costumes.

Aunt Plumy laughed till the tears rolled down her cheeks as the girls compressed her into the plum-colored gown with its short waist, leg-of-mutton sleeves, and narrow skirt. But a worked scarf hid all deficiencies, and the towering cap struck awe into the soul of the most frivolous observer.

"Keep an eye on me, girls, for I shall certainly split somewheres or lose my head-piece off when I'm trottin' round. What would my blessed mother say if she could see me rigged out in her best things?" and with a smile and a sigh the old lady departed to look after "the boys," and see that the supper was all right.

Three prettier damsels never tripped down the wide

staircase than the brilliant brunette in crimson brocade, the pensive blonde in blue, or the rosy little bride in old muslin and white satin.

A gallant court gentleman met them in the hall with a superb bow, and escorted them to the parlor, where Grandma Basset's ghost was discovered dancing with a modern major in full uniform.

Mutual admiration and many compliments followed, till other ancient ladies and gentlemen arrived in all manner of queer costumes, and the old house seemed to wake from its humdrum quietude to sudden music and merriment, as if a past generation had returned to keep its Christmas there.

The village fiddler soon struck up the good old tunes, and then the strangers saw dancing that filled them with mingled mirth and envy; it was so droll, yet so hearty. The young men, unusually awkward in their grandfathers' knee-breeches, flapping vests, and swallow-tail coats, footed it bravely with the buxom girls who were the prettier for their quaintness, and danced with such vigor that their high combs stood awry, their furbelows waved wildly, and their cheeks were as red as their breast-knots, or hose.

It was impossible to stand still, and one after the other

the city folk yielded to the spell, Randal leading off with Ruth, Sophie swept away by Saul, and Emily being taken possession of by a young giant of eighteen, who spun her around with a boyish impetuosity that took her breath away. Even Aunt Plumy was discovered jigging it alone in the pantry, as if the music was too much for her, and the plates and glasses jingled gaily on the shelves in time to Money Musk and Fishers' Hornpipe.

A pause came at last, however, and fans fluttered, heated brows were wiped, jokes were made, lovers exchanged confidences, and every nook and corner held a man and maid carrying on the sweet game which is never out of fashion. There was a glitter of gold lace in the back entry, and a train of blue and primrose shone in the dim light. There was a richer crimson than that of the geraniums in the deep window, and a dainty shoe tapped the bare floor impatiently as the brilliant black eyes looked everywhere for the court gentleman, while their owner listened to the gruff prattle of an enamored boy. But in the upper hall walked a little white ghost as if waiting for some shadowy companion, and when a dark form appeared ran to take its arm, saying, in a tone of soft satisfaction,—

"I was so afraid you wouldn't come!"

"Why did you leave me, Ruth?" answered a manly voice in a tone of surprise, though the small hand slipping from the velvet coat-sleeve was replaced as if it was pleasant to feel it there.

A pause, and then the other voice answered demurely,—

"Because I was afraid my head would be turned by the fine things you were saying."

"It is impossible to help saying what one feels to such an artless little creature as you are. It does me good to admire anything so fresh and sweet, and won't harm you."

"It might if—"

"If what, my daisy?"

"I believed it," and a laugh seemed to finish the broken sentence better than the words.

"You may, Ruth, for I do sincerely admire the most genuine girl I have seen for a long time. And walking here with you in your bridal white I was just asking myself if I should not be a happier man with a home of my own and a little wife hanging on my arm than drifting about the world as I do now with only myself to care for."

"I know you would!" and Ruth spoke so earnestly that

Randal was both touched and startled, fearing he had ventured too far in a mood of unwonted sentiment, born of the romance of the hour and the sweet frankness of his companion.

"Then you don't think it would be rash for some sweet woman to take me in hand and make me happy, since fame is a failure?"

"Oh, no; it would be easy work if she loved you. I know some one—if I only dared to tell her name."

"Upon my soul, this is cool," and Randal looked down, wondering if the audacious lady on his arm could be shy Ruth.

If he had seen the malicious merriment in her eyes he would have been more humiliated still, but they were modestly averted, and the face under the little hat was full of a soft agitation rather dangerous even to a man of the world.

"She is a captivating little creature, but it is too soon for anything but a mild flirtation. I must delay further innocent revelations or I shall do something rash."

While making this excellent resolution Randal had been pressing the hand upon his arm and gently pacing down the dimly lighted hall with the sound of music in his ears, Ruth's sweetest roses in his button-hole, and a loving little girl beside him, as he thought.

"You shall tell me by and by when we are in town. I am sure you will come, and meanwhile don't forget me."

"I am going in the spring, but I shall not be with Sophie," answered Ruth, in a whisper.

"With whom then? I shall long to see you."

"With my husband. I am to be married in May."

"The deuce you are!" escaped Randal, as he stopped short to stare at his companion, sure she was not in earnest.

But she was, for as he looked the sound of steps coming up the back stairs made her whole face flush and brighten with the unmistakable glow of happy love, and she completed Randal's astonishment by running into the arms of the young minister, saying with an irrepressible laugh, "Oh, John, why didn't you come before?"

The court gentleman was all right in a moment, and the coolest of the three as he offered his congratulations and gracefully retired, leaving the lovers to enjoy the tryst he had delayed. But as he went down stairs his brows were knit, and he slapped the broad railing smartly with his cocked hat as if some irritation must find vent in a more energetic way than merely saying, "Confound the little baggage!" under his breath.

Such an amazing supper came from Aunt Plumy's big pantry that the city guests could not eat for laughing at the queer dishes circulating through the rooms, and copiously partaken of by the hearty young folks.

Doughnuts and cheese, pie and pickles, cider and tea, baked beans and custards, cake and cold turkey, bread and butter, plum pudding and French bonbons, Sophie's contribution.

"May I offer you the native delicacies, and share your plate? Both are very good, but the china has run short, and after such vigorous exercise as you have had you must need refreshment. I'm sure I do!" said Randal, bowing before Emily with a great blue platter laden with two doughnuts, two wedges of pumpkin pie and two spoons.

The smile with which she welcomed him, the alacrity with which she made room beside her and seemed to enjoy the supper he brought, was so soothing to his ruffled spirit that he soon began to feel that there is no friend like an old friend, that it would not be difficult to name a sweet woman who would take him in hand and would make him happy if he cared to ask her, and he began to think he would by and by, it was so pleasant to sit in that green corner with waves of crimson brocade flowing over his feet, and a fine face softening beautifully under his eyes.

The supper was not romantic, but the situation was, and Emily found that pie ambrosial food eaten with the man she loved, whose eyes talked more eloquently than the tongue just then busy with a doughnut. Ruth kept away, but glanced at them as she served her company, and her own happy experience helped her to see that all was going well in that quarter. Saul and Sophie emerged from the back entry with shining countenances, but carefully avoided each other for the rest of the evening. No one observed this but Aunt Plumy from the recesses of her pantry, and she folded her hands as if well content, as she murmured fervently over a pan full of crullers, "Bless the dears! Now I can die happy."

Every one thought Sophie's old-fashioned dress immensely becoming, and several of his former men said to Saul with blunt admiration, "Major, you look to-night as you used to after we'd gained a big battle."

"I feel as if I had," answered the splendid Major, with eyes much brighter than his buttons, and a heart under them infinitely prouder than when he was promoted on the field of honor, for his Waterloo was won.

There was more dancing, followed by games, in which Aunt Plumy shone pre-eminent, for the supper was off her mind and she could enjoy herself. There were shouts of merriment as the blithe old lady twirled the platter, hunted the squirrel, and went to Jerusalem like a girl of sixteen; her cap in a ruinous condition, and every seam of the purple dress straining like sails in a gale. It was great fun, but at midnight it came to an end, and the young folks, still bubbling over with innocent jollity, went jingling away along the snowy hills, unanimously pronouncing Mrs. Basset's party the best of the season.

"Never had such a good time in my life!" exclaimed Sophie, as the family stood together in the kitchen where the candles among the wreaths were going out, and the floor was strewn with wrecks of past joy.

"I'm proper glad, dear. Now you all go to bed and lay as late as you like to-morrow. I'm so kinder worked up I couldn't sleep, so Saul and me will put things to rights without a mite of noise to disturb you"; and Aunt Plumy sent them off with a smile that was a benediction, Sophie thought.

"The dear old soul speaks as if midnight was an unheard-of hour for Christians to be up. What would she say if she knew how we seldom go to bed till dawn in the ball season? I'm so wide awake I've half a mind to pack a little. Randal must go at two, he says, and we shall want his escort," said Emily, as the girls laid away their brocades in the press in Sophie's room.

"I'm not going. Aunt can't spare me, and there is nothing to go for yet," answered Sophie, beginning to take the white chrysanthemums out of her pretty hair.

"My dear child, you will die of ennui up here. Very nice for a week or so, but frightful for a winter. We are going to be very gay, and cannot get on without you," cried Emily dismayed at the suggestion.

"You will have to, for I'm not coming. I am very happy here, and so tired of the frivolous life I lead in town, that I have decided to try a better one," and Sophie's mirror reflected a face full of the sweetest content.

"Have you lost your mind? experienced religion? or any other dreadful thing? You always were odd, but this last freak is the strangest of all. What will your guardian say, and the world?" added Emily in the awe-stricken tone of one who stood in fear of the omnipotent Mrs. Grundy.

"Guardy will be glad to be rid of me, and I don't care that for the world," cried Sophie, snapping her fingers with a joyful sort of recklessness which completed Emily's bewilderment.

"But Mr. Hammond? Are you going to throw away millions, lose your chance of making the best match in the city, and driving the girls of our set out of their wits with envy?"

Sophie laughed at her friend's despairing cry, and turning round said quietly,—

"I wrote to Mr. Hammond last night, and this evening received my reward for being an honest girl. Saul and I are to be married in the spring when Ruth is."

Emily fell prone upon the bed as if the announcement was too much for her, but was up again in an instant to declare with prophetic solemnity,—

"I knew something was going on, but hoped to get you away before you were lost. Sophie, you will repent. Be warned, and forget this sad delusion."

"Too late for that. The pang I suffered yesterday when I thought Saul was dead showed me how well I loved him. To-night he asked me to stay, and no power in the world can part us. Oh! Emily, it is all so sweet, so beautiful, that *everything* is possible, and I know I shall be happy in this dear old home, full of love and peace and honest hearts. I only hope you may find as true and tender a man to live for as my Saul."

Sophie's face was more eloquent than her fervent words, and Emily beautifully illustrated the inconsistency of her sex by suddenly embracing her friend, with the incoherent exclamation, "I think I have, dear! Your brave Saul is worth a dozen old Hammonds, and I do believe you are right."

It is unnecessary to tell how, as if drawn by the irresistible magic of sympathy, Ruth and her mother crept in one by one to join the midnight conference and add their smiles and tears, tender hopes and proud delight to the joys of that memorable hour. Nor how Saul, unable to sleep, mounted guard below, and meeting Randal prowling down to soothe his nerves with a surreptitious cigar found it impossible to help confiding to his attentive ear the happiness that would break bounds and overflow in unusual eloquence.

Peace fell upon the old house at last, and all slept as if some magic herb had touched their eyelids, bringing blissful dreams and a glad awakening.

"Can't we persuade you to come with us, Miss Sophie?" asked Randal next day, as they made their adieux.

"I'm under orders now, and dare not disobey my superior officer," answered Sophie, handing her Major his driving gloves, with a look which plainly showed that she had joined the great army of devoted women who enlist for life and ask no pay but love.

"I shall depend on being invited to your wedding, then, and yours, too, Miss Ruth," added Randal, shaking hands with "the little baggage," as if he had quite forgiven her mockery and forgotten his own brief lapse into sentiment.

Before she could reply Aunt Plumy said, in a tone of calm conviction, that made them all laugh, and some of them look conscious,—

"Spring is a good time for weddin's, and I shouldn't wonder ef there was quite a number."

"Nor I"; and Saul and Sophie smiled at one another as they saw how carefully Randal arranged Emily's wraps.

Then with kisses, thanks and all the good wishes that happy hearts could imagine, the guests drove away, to remember long and gratefully that pleasant country Christmas.

L. M. Montgomery

1874–1942

CHRISTMAS AT RED BUTTE

"Of course Santa Claus will come," said Jimmy Martin confidently. Jimmy was ten, and at ten it is easy to be confident. "Why, he's *got* to come because it is Christmas Eve, and he always *has* come. You know that, twins."

Yes, the twins knew it and, cheered by Jimmy's superior wisdom, their doubts passed away. There had been one terrible moment when Theodora had sighed and told them they mustn't be too much disappointed if Santa Claus did not come this year because the crops had been poor, and he mightn't have had enough presents to go around.

"That doesn't make any difference to Santa Claus," scoffed Jimmy. "You know as well as I do, Theodora Prentice, that Santa Claus is rich whether the crops fail or not. They failed three years ago, before Father died, but Santa Claus came all the same. Prob'bly you don't remember it, twins, 'cause you were too little, but I do. Of course he'll come, so don't you worry a mite. And he'll bring my skates and your dolls. He knows we're expecting them, Theodora, 'cause we wrote him a letter last week, and threw it up the chimney. And there'll be candy and nuts, of course, and Mother's gone to town to buy a turkey. I tell you we're going to have a ripping Christmas."

"Well, don't use such slangy words about it, Jimmy-boy," sighed Theodora. She couldn't bear to dampen their hopes any further, and perhaps Aunt Elizabeth might manage it if the colt sold well. But Theodora had her painful doubts, and she sighed again as she looked out of the window far down the trail that wound across the prairie, red-lighted by the declining sun of the short wintry afternoon.

"Do people always sigh like that when they get to be sixteen?" asked Jimmy curiously. "You didn't sigh like that when you were only fifteen, Theodora. I wish you wouldn't. It makes me feel funny—and it's not a nice kind of funniness either."

"It's a bad habit I've got into lately," said Theodora,

trying to laugh. "Old folks are dull sometimes, you know, Jimmy-boy."

"Sixteen *is* awful old, isn't it?" said Jimmy reflectively. "I'll tell you what *I'm* going to do when I'm sixteen, Theodora. I'm going to pay off the mortgage, and buy mother a silk dress, and a piano for the twins. Won't that be elegant? I'll be able to do that 'cause I'm a man. Of course if I was only a girl I couldn't."

"I hope you'll be a good kind brave man and a real help to your mother," said Theodora softly, sitting down before the cosy fire and lifting the fat little twins into her lap.

"Oh, I'll be good to her, never you fear," assured Jimmy, squatting comfortably down on the little fur rug before the stove—the skin of the coyote his father had killed four years ago. "I believe in being good to your mother when you've only got the one. Now tell us a story, Theodora—a real jolly story, you know, with lots of fighting in it. Only please don't kill anybody. I like to hear about fighting, but I like to have all the people come out alive."

Theodora laughed, and began a story about the Riel Rebellion of '85—a story which had the double merit of being true and exciting at the same time. It was quite dark when she finished, and the twins were nodding, but Jimmy's eyes were wide open and sparkling.

"That was great," he said, drawing a long breath. "Tell us another."

"No, it's bedtime for you all," said Theodora firmly. "One story at a time is my rule, you know."

"But I want to sit up till Mother comes home," objected Jimmy.

"You can't. She may be very late, for she would have to wait to see Mr. Porter. Besides, you don't know what time Santa Claus might come—if he comes at all. If he were to drive along and see you children up instead of being sound asleep in bed, he might go right on and never call at all."

This argument was too much for Jimmy.

"All right, we'll go. But we have to hang up our stockings first. Twins, get yours."

The twins toddled off in great excitement, and brought back their Sunday stockings, which Jimmy proceeded to hang along the edge of the mantel shelf. This done, they all trooped obediently off to bed. Theodora gave another sigh, and seated herself at the window, where she could watch the moonlit prairie for Mrs. Martin's homecoming and knit at the same time.

I am afraid that you will think from all the sighing Theodora was doing that she was a very melancholy and despondent young lady. You couldn't think anything more unlike the real Theodora. She was the jolliest, bravest girl of sixteen in all Saskatchewan, as her shining brown eyes and rosy, dimpled cheeks would have told you; and her sighs were not on her own account, but simply for fear the children were going to be disappointed. She knew that they would be almost heartbroken if Santa Claus did not come, and that this would hurt the patient hardworking little mother more than all else.

Five years before this, Theodora had come to live with Uncle George and Aunt Elizabeth in the little log house at Red Butte. Her own mother had just died, and Theodora had only her big brother Donald left, and Donald had Klondike fever. The Martins were poor, but they had gladly made room for their little niece, and Theodora had lived there ever since, her aunt's right-hand girl and the beloved playmate of the children. They had been very happy until Uncle George's death two years before this Christmas Eve; but since then there had been hard times in the little log house, and though Mrs. Martin and Theodora did their best, it was a woefully hard task to make both ends meet, especially this year when their crops had been poor. Theodora and her aunt had made every sacrifice possible for the children's sake, and at least Jimmy and the twins had not felt the pinch very severely yet.

At seven Mrs. Martin's bells jingled at the door and Theodora flew out. "Go right in and get warm, Auntie," she said briskly. "I'll take Ned away and unharness him."

"It's a bitterly cold night," said Mrs. Martin wearily. There was a note of discouragement in her voice that struck dismay to Theodora's heart.

"I'm afraid it means no Christmas for the children tomorrow," she thought sadly, as she led Ned away to the stable. When she returned to the kitchen Mrs. Martin was sitting by the fire, her face in her chilled hand, sobbing convulsively.

"Auntie—oh, Auntie, don't!" exclaimed Theodora impulsively. It was such a rare thing to see her plucky, resolute little aunt in tears. "You're cold and tired—I'll have a nice cup of tea for you in a trice."

"No, it isn't that," said Mrs. Martin brokenly. "It was seeing those stockings hanging there. Theodora, I couldn't get a thing for the children—not a single thing. Mr. Porter would only give forty dollars for the colt, and when all the bills were paid there was barely enough left for such necessaries as we must have. I suppose I ought to feel thankful I could get those. But the thought of the children's disappointment tomorrow is more than I can bear. It would have been better to have told them long ago, but I kept building on getting more for the colt. Well, it's weak and foolish to give way like this. We'd better both take a cup of tea and go to bed. It will save fuel."

When Theodora went up to her little room her face was very thoughtful. She took a small box from her table and carried it to the window. In it was a very pretty little gold locket hung on a narrow blue ribbon. Theodora held it tenderly in her fingers, and looked out over the moonlit prairie with a very sober face. Could she give up her dear locket— the locket Donald had given her just before he started for the Klondike? She had never thought she could do such a thing. It was almost the only thing she had to remind her of Donald—handsome, merry, impulsive, warmhearted Donald, who had gone away four years ago with a smile on his bonny face and splendid hope in his heart.

"Here's a locket for you, Gift o' God," he had said gaily—he had such a dear loving habit of calling her by the beautiful meaning of her name. A lump came into Theodora's throat as she remembered it. "I couldn't afford a chain too, but when I come back I'll bring you a rope of Klondike nuggets for it."

Then he had gone away. For two years letters had come from him regularly. Then he wrote that he had joined a prospecting party to a remote wilderness. After that was silence, deepening into anguish of suspense that finally ended in hopelessness. A rumour came that Donald Prentice was dead. None had returned from the expedition he had joined. Theodora had long ago given up all hope of ever seeing Donald again. Hence her locket was doubly dear to her.

But Aunt Elizabeth had always been so good and loving and kind to her. Could she not make the sacrifice for her sake? Yes, she could and would. Theodora flung up her head with a gesture that meant decision. She took out of the locket the bits of hair—her mother's and Donald's—which it contained (perhaps a tear or two fell as she did so) and then hastily donned her warmest cap and wraps. It was only three miles to Spencer; she could easily walk it in an hour and, as it was Christmas Eve, the shops would be open late. She muse walk, for Ned could not be taken out again, and the mare's foot was sore. Besides, Aunt Elizabeth must not know until it was done.

As stealthily as if she were bound on some nefarious errand, Theodora slipped downstairs and out of the house. The next minute she was hurrying along the trail in the moonlight. The great dazzling prairie was around her, the mystery and splendour of the northern night all about her. It was very calm and cold, but Theodora walked so briskly that she kept warm. The trail from Red Butte to Spencer was a lonely one. Mr. Lurgan's house, halfway to town, was the only dwelling on it.

When Theodora reached Spencer she made her way at once to the only jewellery store the little town contained. Mr. Benson, its owner, had been a friend of her uncle's, and Theodora felt sure that he would buy her locket. Nevertheless her heart beat quickly, and her breath came and went uncomfortably fast as she went in. Suppose he wouldn't buy it. Then there would be no Christmas for the children at Red Butte.

"Good evening, Miss Theodora," said Mr. Benson briskly. "What can I do for you?"

"I'm afraid I'm not a very welcome sort of customer, Mr. Benson," said Theodora, with an uncertain smile. "I want to sell, not buy. Could you—will you buy this locket?"

Mr. Benson pursed up his lips, took up the locket, and examined it. "Well, I don't often buy second-hand stuff," he said, after some reflection, "but I don't mind obliging you, Miss Theodora. I'll give you four dollars for this trinket."

Theodora knew the locket had cost a great deal more than that, but four dollars would get what she wanted, and she dared not ask for more. In a few minutes the locket was in Mr. Benson's possession, and Theodora, with four crisp new bills in her purse, was hurrying to the toy store. Half an hour later she was on her way back to Red Butte, with as many parcels as she could carry—Jimmy's skates, two lovely dolls for the twins, packages of nuts and candy, and a nice plump turkey. Theodora beguiled her lonely tramp by picturing the children's joy in the morning.

About a quarter of a mile past Mr. Lurgan's house the trail curved suddenly about a bluff of poplars. As Theodora rounded the turn she halted in amazement. Almost at her feet the body of a man was lying across the road. He was clad in a big fur coat, and had a fur cap pulled well down over his forehead and ears. Almost all of him that could be seen was a full bushy beard. Theodora had no idea who he was, or where he had come from. But she realized that he was unconscious, and that he would speedily freeze to death if help were not brought. The footprints of a horse galloping across the prairie suggested a fall and a runaway, but Theodora did not waste time in speculation. She ran back at full speed to Mr. Lurgan's, and roused the household. In a few minutes Mr. Lurgan and his son had hitched a horse to a wood-sleigh, and hurried down the trail to the unfortunate man.

Theodora, knowing that her assistance was not needed, and that she ought to get home as quickly as possible, went on her way as soon as she had seen the stranger in safe keeping. When she reached the little log house she crept in, cautiously put the children's gifts in their stockings, placed the turkey on the table where Aunt Elizabeth would see it the first thing in the morning, and then slipped off to bed, a very weary but very happy girl.

The joy that reigned in the little log house the next day more than repaid Theodora for her sacrifice.

"Whoopee, didn't I tell you that Santa Claus would come all right!" shouted the delighted Jimmy. "Oh, what splendid skates!"

The twins hugged their dolls in silent rapture, but Aunt Elizabeth's face was the best of all.

Then the dinner had to be prepared, and everybody had a hand in that. Just as Theodora, after a grave peep into the oven, had announced that the turkey was done, a sleigh dashed around the house. Theodora flew to answer the knock at the door, and there stood Mr. Lurgan and a big, bewhiskered, fur-coated fellow whom Theodora recognized as the stranger she had found on the trail. But—*was* he a stranger? There was something oddly familiar in those merry brown eyes. Theodora felt herself growing dizzy.

"Donald!" she gasped. "Oh, Donald!"

And then she was in the big fellow's arms, laughing and crying at the same time.

Donald it was indeed. And then followed half an hour during which everybody talked at once, and the turkey would have been burned to a crisp had it not been for the presence of mind of Mr. Lurgan who, being the least excited of them all, took it out of the oven, and set it on the back of the stove.

"To think that it was you last night, and that I never dreamed it," exclaimed Theodora. "Oh, Donald, if I hadn't gone to town!"

"I'd have frozen to death, I'm afraid," said Donald soberly. "I got into Spencer on the last train last night. I felt that I must come right out—I couldn't wait till morning. But there wasn't a team to be got for love or money—it was Christmas Eve and all the livery rigs were out. So I came on horseback. Just by that bluff something frightened my horse, and he shied violently. I was half asleep and thinking of my little sister, and I went off like a shot. I suppose I struck my head against a tree. Anyway, I knew nothing more until I came to in Mr. Lurgan's kitchen. I wasn't much hurt—feel none the worse of it except for a sore head and shoulder. But, oh, Gift o' God, how you have grown! I can't realize that you are the little sister I left four years ago. I suppose you have been thinking I was dead?"

"Yes, and, oh, Donald, where *have* you been?"

"Well, I went way up north with a prospecting party. We had a tough time the first year, I can tell you, and some of us never came back. We weren't in a country where post offices were lying round loose either, you see. Then at last, just as we were about giving up in despair, we struck it rich. I've brought a snug little pile home with me, and things are going to look up in this log house, Gift o' God. There'll be no more worrying for you dear people over mortgages."

"I'm so glad—for Auntie's sake," said Theodora, with shining eyes. "But, oh, Donald, it's best of all just to have you back. I'm so perfectly happy that I don't know what to do or say."

"Well, I think you might have dinner," said Jimmy in an injured tone. "The turkey's getting stone cold, and I'm most starving. I just can't stand it another minute."

So, with a laugh, they all sat down to the table and ate the merriest Christmas dinner the little log house had ever known.

A CHRISTMAS INSPIRATION

"Well, I really think Santa Claus has been very good to us all," said Jean Lawrence, pulling the pins out of her heavy coil of fair hair and letting it ripple over her shoulders.

"So do I," said Nellie Preston as well as she could with a mouthful of chocolates. "Those blessed home folks of mine seem to have divined by instinct the very things I most wanted."

It was the dusk of Christmas Eve and they were all in Jean Lawrence's room at No. 16 Chestnut Terrace. No. 16 was a boarding-house, and boarding-houses are not pro-verbially cheerful places in which to spend Christmas, but Jean's room, at least, was a pleasant spot, and all the girls had brought their Christmas presents in to show each other.

Christmas came on Sunday that year and the Saturday evening mail at Chestnut Terrace had been an exciting one.

Jean had lighted the pink-globed lamp on her table and the mellow light fell over merry faces as the girls chatted about their gifts. On the table was a big white box heaped with roses that betokened a bit of Christmas extravagance on somebody's part. Jean's brother had sent them to her from Montreal, and all the girls were enjoying them in common.

No. 16 Chestnut Terrace was overrun with girls generally. But just now only five were left; all the others had gone home for Christmas, but these five could not go and were bent on making the best of it.

Belle and Olive Reynolds, who were sitting on the bed—Jean could never keep them off it—were High School girls; they were said to be always laughing, and even the fact that they could not go home for Christmas because a young brother had measles did not dampen their spirits.

Beth Hamilton, who was hovering over the roses, and Nellie Preston, who was eating candy, were art students, and their homes were too far away to visit. As for Jean Lawrence, she was an orphan, and had no home of her own. She worked on the staff of one of the big city newspapers and the other girls were a little in awe of her cleverness, but her nature was a "chummy" one and her room was a favourite rendezvous. Everybody liked frank, open-handed and -hearted Jean.

"It was so funny to see the postman when he came this evening," said Olive. "He just bulged with parcels. They were sticking out in every direction."

"We all got our share of them," said Jean with a sigh of content.

"Even the cook got six—I counted."

"Miss Allen didn't get a thing—not even a letter," said Beth quickly. Beth had a trick of seeing things that other girls didn't.

"I forgot Miss Allen. No, I don't believe she did," answered Jean thoughtfully as she twisted up her pretty hair. "How dismal it must be to be so forlorn as that on Christmas Eve of all times. Ugh! I'm glad I have friends."

"I saw Miss Allen watching us as we opened our parcels and letters," Beth went on. "I happened to look up once, and such an expression as was on her face, girls! It was pathetic and sad and envious all at once. It really made me feel bad— for five minutes," she concluded honestly.

"Hasn't Miss Allen any friends at all?" asked Beth.

"No, I don't think she has," answered Jean. "She has lived here for fourteen years, so Mrs. Pickrell says. Think of that, girls! Fourteen years at Chestnut Terrace! Is it any wonder that she is thin and dried-up and snappy?"

"Nobody ever comes to see her and she never goes anywhere," said Beth. "Dear me! She must feel lonely now when everybody else is being remembered by their friends. I can't forget her face tonight; it actually haunts me. Girls, how would you feel if you hadn't anyone belonging to you, and if nobody thought about you at Christmas?"

"Ow!" said Olive, as if the mere idea made her shiver.

A little silence followed. To tell the truth, none of them liked Miss Allen. They knew that she did not like them either, but considered them frivolous and pert, and complained when they made a racket.

"The skeleton at the feast," Jean called her, and certainly the presence of the pale, silent, discontented-looking woman at the No. 16 table did not tend to heighten its festivity.

Presently Jean said with a dramatic flourish, "Girls, I have an inspiration—a Christmas inspiration!"

"What is it?" cried four voices.

"Just this. Let us give Miss Allen a Christmas surprise. She has not received a single present and I'm sure she feels lonely. Just think how we would feel if we were in her place."

"That is true," said Olive thoughtfully. "Do you know, girls, this evening I went to her room with a message from Mrs. Pickrell, and I do believe she had been crying. Her room looked dreadfully bare and cheerless, too. I think she is very poor. What are we to do, Jean?"

"Let us each give her something nice. We can put the things just outside of her door so that she will see them whenever she opens it. I'll give her some of Fred's roses too, and I'll write a Christmassy letter in my very best style to go with them," said Jean, warming up to her ideas as she talked.

The other girls caught her spirit and entered into the plan with enthusiasm.

"Splendid!" cried Beth. "Jean, it is an inspiration, sure enough. Haven't we been horribly selfish—thinking of nothing but our own gifts and fun and pleasure? I really feel ashamed."

"Let us do the thing up the very best way we can," said

Nellie, forgetting even her beloved chocolates in her eagerness. "The shops are open yet. Let us go up town and invest."

Five minutes later five capped and jacketed figures were
scurrying up the street in the frosty, starlit December dusk.
Miss Allen in her cold little room heard their gay voices
and sighed. She was crying by herself in the dark. It was
Christmas for everybody but her, she thought drearily.

In an hour the girls came back with their purchases.

"Now, let's hold a council of war," said Jean jubilantly.
"I hadn't the faintest idea what Miss Allen would like so
I just guessed wildly. I got her a lace handkerchief and a
big bottle of perfume and a painted photograph frame—
and I'll stick my own photo in it for fun. That was really
all I could afford. Christmas purchases have left my purse
dreadfully lean."

"I got her a glove-box and a pin tray," said Belle, "and
Olive got her a calendar and Whittier's poems. And besides
we are going to give her half of that big plummy fruit cake
Mother sent us from home. I'm sure she hasn't tasted anything so delicious for years, for fruit cakes don't grow on
Chestnut Terrace and she never goes anywhere else for
a meal."

Beth had bought a pretty cup and saucer and said she meant to give one of her pretty water-colours too. Nellie, true to her reputation, had invested in a big box of chocolate creams, a gorgeously striped candy cane, a bag of oranges, and a brilliant lampshade of rose-coloured crepe paper to top off with.

"It makes such a lot of show for the money," she explained. "I am bankrupt, like Jean."

"Well, we've got a lot of pretty things," said Jean in a tone of satisfaction. "Now we must do them up nicely. Will you wrap them in tissue paper, girls, and tie them with baby ribbon—here's a box of it—while I write that letter?"

While the others chatted over their parcels Jean wrote her letter, and Jean could write delightful letters. She had a decided talent in that respect, and her correspondents all declared her letters to be things of beauty and joy forever. She put her best into Miss Allen's Christmas letter. Since then she has written many bright and clever things, but I do not believe she ever in her life wrote anything more genuinely original and delightful than that letter. Besides, it breathed the very spirit of Christmas, and all the girls declared that it was splendid.

"You must all sign it now," said Jean, "and I'll put it in one of those big envelopes; and, Nellie, won't you write her name on it in fancy letters?"

Which Nellie proceeded to do, and furthermore embellished the envelope by a border of chubby cherubs, dancing hand in hand around it and a sketch of No. 16 Chestnut Terrace in the corner in lieu of a stamp. Not content with this she hunted out a huge sheet of drawing paper and drew upon it an original pen-and-ink design after her own heart. A dudish cat—Miss Allen was fond of the No. 16 cat if she could be said to be fond of anything—was portrayed seated on a rocker arrayed in smoking jacket and cap with a cigar waved airily aloft in one paw while the other held out a placard bearing the legend "Merry Christmas." A second cat in full street costume bowed politely, hat in paw, and waved a banner inscribed with "Happy New Year," while faintly suggested kittens gambolled around the border. The girls laughed until they cried over it and voted it to be the best thing Nellie had yet done in original work.

All this had taken time and it was past eleven o'clock. Miss Allen had cried herself to sleep long ago and everybody else in Chestnut Terrace was abed when five figures cautiously crept down the hall, headed by Jean with a dim lamp. Outside of Miss Allen's door the procession halted and the girls silently arranged their gifts on the floor.

"That's done," whispered Jean in a tone of satisfaction as they tiptoed back. "And now let us go to bed or Mrs. Pickrell, bless her heart, will be down on us for burning so much midnight oil. Oil has gone up, you know, girls."

It was in the early morning that Miss Allen opened her door. But early as it was, another door down the hall was half open too and five rosy faces were peering cautiously out. The girls had been up for an hour for fear they would miss the sight and were all in Nellie's room, which commanded a view of Miss Allen's door.

That lady's face was a study. Amazement, incredulity, wonder, chased each other over it, succeeded by a glow of pleasure. On the floor before her was a snug little pyramid of parcels topped by Jean's letter. On a chair behind it was a bowl of delicious hot-house roses and Nellie's placard.

Miss Allen looked down the hall but saw nothing, for Jean had slammed the door just in time. Half an hour later when they were going down to breakfast Miss Allen came along the hall with outstretched hands to meet them. She had been crying again, but I think her tears were happy ones; and she was smiling now. A cluster of Jean's roses were pinned on her breast.

"Oh, girls, girls," she said, with a little tremble in her voice, "I can never thank you enough. It was so kind and sweet of you. You don't know how much good you have done me."

Breakfast was an unusually cheerful affair at No. 16 that morning. There was no skeleton at the feast and everybody was beaming. Miss Allen laughed and talked like a girl herself.

"Oh, how surprised I was!" she said. "The roses were like a bit of summer, and those cats of Nellie's were so funny and delightful. And your letter too, Jean! I cried and laughed over it. I shall read it every day for a year."

After breakfast everyone went to Christmas service. The girls went uptown to the church they attended. The city was very beautiful in the morning sunshine. There had been a white frost in the night and the tree-lined avenues and public squares seemed like glimpses of fairyland.

"How lovely the world is," said Jean.

"This is really the very happiest Christmas morning I

have ever known," declared Nellie. "I never felt so really Christmassy in my inmost soul before."

"I suppose," said Beth thoughtfully, "that it is because we have discovered for ourselves the old truth that it is more blessed to give than to receive. I've always known it, in a way, but I never realized it before."

"Blessing on Jean's Christmas inspiration," said Nellie. "But, girls, let us try to make it an all-the-year-round inspiration, I say. We can bring a little of our own sunshine into Miss Allen's life as long as we live with her."

"Amen to that!" said Jean heartily. "Oh, listen, girls— the Christmas chimes!"

And over all the beautiful city was wafted the grand old message of peace on earth and good will to all the world.

A CHRISTMAS MISTAKE

"Tomorrow is Christmas," announced Teddy Grant exultantly, as he sat on the floor struggling manfully with a refractory bootlace that was knotted and tagless and stubbornly refused to go into the eyelets of Teddy's patched boots. "Ain't I glad, though. Hurrah!"

His mother was washing the breakfast dishes in a dreary, listless sort of way. She looked tired and broken-spirited. Ted's enthusiasm seemed to grate on her, for she answered sharply:

"Christmas, indeed. I can't see that it is anything for us to rejoice over. Other people may be glad enough, but what with winter coming on I'd sooner it was spring than Christmas. Mary Alice, do lift that child out of the ashes and put its shoes and stockings on. Everything seems to be at sixes and sevens here this morning."

Keith, the oldest boy, was coiled up on the sofa calmly working out some algebra problems, quite oblivious to the noise around him. But he looked up from his slate, with his pencil suspended above an obstinate equation, to declaim with a flourish:

"Christmas comes but once a year,
And then Mother wishes it wasn't here."

"I don't, then," said Gordon, son number two, who was preparing his own noon lunch of bread and molasses at the table, and making an atrocious mess of crumbs and sugary syrup over everything. "I know one thing to be thankful for, and that is that there'll be no school. We'll have a whole week of holidays."

Gordon was noted for his aversion to school and his affection for holidays.

"And we're going to have turkey for dinner," declared Teddy, getting up off the floor and rushing to secure his share of bread and molasses, "and cranb'ry sauce and—and—pound cake! Ain't we, Ma?"

"No, you are not," said Mrs. Grant desperately, dropping the dishcloth and snatching the baby on her knee to wipe the crust of cinders and molasses from the chubby pink-and-white face. "You may as well know it now, children, I've kept it from you so far in hopes that something would turn up, but nothing has. We can't have any Christmas dinner tomorrow—we can't afford it. I've pinched and saved every way I could for the last month, hoping that I'd be able to get a turkey for you anyhow, but you'll have to do without it. There's that doctor's bill to pay and a dozen other bills coming in—and people say they can't wait. I suppose they can't, but it's kind of hard, I must say."

The little Grants stood with open mouths and horrified eyes. No turkey for Christmas! Was the world coming to an end? Wouldn't the government interfere if anyone ventured to dispense with a Christmas celebration?

The gluttonous Teddy stuffed his fists into his eyes and lifted up his voice. Keith, who understood better than the others the look on his mother's face, took his blubbering young brother by the collar and marched him into the porch. The twins, seeing the summary proceeding, swallowed the outcries they had intended to make, although they couldn't keep a few big tears from running down their fat cheeks.

Mrs. Grant looked pityingly at the disappointed faces about her.

"Don't cry, children, you make me feel worse. We are not the only ones who will have to do without a Christmas turkey. We ought to be very thankful that we have anything to eat at all. I hate to disappoint you, but it can't be helped."

"Never mind, Mother," said Keith, comfortingly, relaxing his hold upon the porch door, whereupon it suddenly flew open and precipitated Teddy, who had been tugging at the handle, heels over head backwards. "We know you've done your best. It's been a hard year for you. Just wait, though. I'll soon be grown up, and then you and these greedy youngsters shall feast on turkey every day of the year. Hello, Teddy, have you got on your feet again? Mind, sir, no more blubbering!"

"When I'm a man," announced Teddy with dignity, "I'd just like to see you put me in the porch. And I mean to have turkey all the time and I won't give you any, either."

"All right, you greedy small boy. Only take yourself off to school now, and let us hear no more squeaks out of you. Tramp, all of you, and give Mother a chance to get her work done."

Mrs. Grant got up and fell to work at her dishes with a brighter face.

"Well, we mustn't give in; perhaps things will be better

after a while. I'll make a famous bread pudding, and you can boil some molasses taffy and ask those little Smithsons next door to help you pull it. They won't whine for turkey, I'll be bound. I don't suppose they ever tasted such a thing in all their lives. If I could afford it, I'd have had them all in to dinner with us. That sermon Mr. Evans preached last Sunday kind of stirred me up. He said we ought always to try and share our Christmas joy with some poor souls who had never learned the meaning of the word. I can't do as much as I'd like to. It was different when your father was alive."

The noisy group grew silent as they always did when their father was spoken of. He had died the year before, and since his death the little family had had a hard time. Keith, to hide his feelings, began to hector the rest.

"Mary Alice, do hurry up. Here, you twin nuisances, get off to school. If you don't you'll be late and then the master will give you a whipping."

"He won't," answered the irrepressible Teddy. "He never whips us, he doesn't. He stands us on the floor sometimes, though," he added, remembering the many times his own chubby legs had been seen to better advantage on the school platform.

"That man," said Mrs. Grant, alluding to the teacher, "makes me nervous. He is the most abstracted creature I ever saw in my life. It is a wonder to me he doesn't walk straight into the river some day. You'll meet him meandering along the street, gazing into vacancy, and he'll never see you nor hear a word you say half the time."

"Yesterday," said Gordon, chuckling over the remembrance, "he came in with a big piece of paper he'd picked up on the entry floor in one hand and his hat in the other— and he stuffed his hat into the coal-scuttle and hung up the paper on a nail as grave as you please. Never knew the difference till Ned Slocum went and told him. He's always doing things like that."

Keith had collected his books and now marched his brothers and sisters off to school. Left alone with the baby, Mrs. Grant betook herself to her work with a heavy heart. But a second interruption broke the progress of her dish-washing.

"I declare," she said, with a surprised glance through the window, "if there isn't that absent-minded schoolteacher coming through the yard! What can he want? Dear me, I do hope Teddy hasn't been cutting capers in school again."

For the teacher's last call had been in October and had

been occasioned by the fact that the irrepressible Teddy would persist in going to school with his pockets filled with live crickets and in driving them harnessed to strings up and down the aisle when the teacher's back was turned. All mild methods of punishment having failed, the teacher had called to talk it over with Mrs. Grant, with the happy result that Teddy's behaviour had improved—in the matter of crickets at least.

But it was about time for another outbreak. Teddy had been unnaturally good for too long a time. Poor Mrs. Grant feared that it was the calm before a storm, and it was with nervous haste that she went to the door and greeted the young teacher.

He was a slight, pale, boyish-looking fellow, with an abstracted, musing look in his large dark eyes. Mrs. Grant noticed with amusement that he wore a white straw hat in spite of the season. His eyes were directed to her face with his usual unseeing gaze.

"Just as though he was looking through me at something a thousand miles away," said Mrs. Grant afterwards. "I believe he was, too. His body was right there on the step before me, but where his soul was is more than you or I or anybody can tell."

"Good morning," he said absently. "I have just called on my way to school with a message from Miss Millar. She wants you all to come up and have Christmas dinner with her tomorrow."

"For the land's sake!" said Mrs. Grant blankly. "I don't understand." To herself she thought, "I wish I dared take him and shake him to find if he's walking in his sleep or not."

"You and all the children—every one," went on the teacher dreamily, as if he were reciting a lesson learned beforehand. "She told me to tell you to be sure and come. Shall I say that you will?"

"Oh, yes, that is—I suppose—I don't know," said Mrs. Grant incoherently. "I never expected—yes, you may tell her we'll come," she concluded abruptly.

"Thank you," said the abstracted messenger, gravely lifting his hat and looking squarely through Mrs. Grant into unknown regions. When he had gone Mrs. Grant went in and sat down, laughing in a sort of hysterical way.

"I wonder if it is all right. Could Cornelia really have told him? She must, I suppose, but it is enough to take one's breath."

Mrs. Grant and Cornelia Millar were cousins, and had

once been the closest of friends, but that was years ago, before some spiteful reports and ill-natured gossip had come between them, making only a little rift at first that soon widened into a chasm of coldness and alienation. Therefore this invitation surprised Mrs. Grant greatly.

Miss Cornelia was a maiden lady of certain years, with a comfortable bank account and a handsome, old-fashioned house on the hill behind the village. She always boarded the schoolteachers and looked after them maternally; she was an active church worker and a tower of strength to struggling ministers and their families.

"If Cornelia has seen fit at last to hold out the hand of reconciliation I'm glad enough to take it. Dear knows, I've wanted to make up often enough, but I didn't think she ever would. We've both of us got too much pride and stubbornness. It's the Turner blood in us that does it. The Turners were all so set. But I mean to do my part now she has done hers."

And Mrs. Grant made a final attack on the dishes with a beaming face.

When the little Grants came home and heard the news, Teddy stood on his head to express his delight, the twins kissed each other, and Mary Alice and Gordon danced around the kitchen.

Keith thought himself too big to betray any joy over a Christmas dinner, but he whistled while doing the chores until the bare welkin in the yard rang, and Teddy, in spite of unheard of misdemeanours, was not collared off into the porch once.

When the young teacher got home from school that evening he found the yellow house full of all sorts of delectable odours. Miss Cornelia herself was concocting mince pies after the famous family recipe, while her ancient and faithful handmaiden, Hannah, was straining into moulds the cranberry jelly. The open pantry door revealed a tempting array of Christmas delicacies.

"Did you call and invite the Smithsons up to dinner as I told you?" asked Miss Cornelia anxiously.

"Yes," was the dreamy response as he glided through the kitchen and vanished into the hall.

Miss Cornelia crimped the edges of her pies delicately with a relieved air. "I made certain he'd forget it," she said. "You just have to watch him as if he were a mere child. Didn't I catch him yesterday starting off to school in his carpet slippers? And in spite of me he got away today in that ridiculous summer hat. You'd better set that jelly in the out-pantry to cool, Hannah; it looks good. We'll give those poor little Smithsons a feast for once in their lives if they never get another."

At this juncture the hall door flew open and Mr. Palmer appeared on the threshold. He seemed considerably agitated and for once his eyes had lost their look of space-searching.

"Miss Millar, I am afraid I did make a mistake this morning—it has just dawned on me. I am almost sure that I called at Mrs. Grant's and invited her and her family instead of the Smithsons. And she said they would come."

Miss Cornelia's face was a study.

"Mr. Palmer," she said, flourishing her crimping fork tragically, "do you mean to say you went and invited Linda Grant here tomorrow? Linda Grant, of all women in this world!"

"I did," said the teacher with penitent wretchedness. "It was very careless of me—I am very sorry. What can I do? I'll go down and tell them I made a mistake if you like."

"You can't do that," groaned Miss Cornelia, sitting down and wrinkling up her forehead in dire perplexity.

"It would never do in the world. For pity's sake, let me think for a minute."

Miss Cornelia did think—to good purpose evidently, for her forehead smoothed out as her meditations proceeded and her face brightened. Then she got up briskly. "Well, you've done it and no mistake. I don't know that I'm sorry, either. Anyhow, we'll leave it as it is. But you must go straight down now and invite the Smithsons too. And for pity's sake, don't make any more mistakes."

When he had gone Miss Cornelia opened her heart to Hannah. "I never could have done it myself—never; the Turner is too strong in me. But I'm glad it is done. I've been wanting for years to make up with Linda. And now the chance has come, thanks to that blessed blundering boy, I mean to make the most of it. Mind, Hannah, you never whisper a word about its being a mistake. Linda must never know. Poor Linda! She's had a hard time. Hannah, we must make some more pies, and I must go straight down to the store and get some more Santa Claus stuff; I've only got enough to go around the Smithsons."

When Mrs. Grant and her family arrived at the yellow house next morning Miss Cornelia herself ran out bareheaded to meet them. The two women shook hands a little stiffly and then a rill of long-repressed affection trickled out from some secret spring in Miss Cornelia's heart and she kissed her new-found old friend tenderly. Linda returned the kiss warmly, and both felt that the old-time friendship was theirs again.

The little Smithsons all came and they and the little Grants sat down on the long bright dining room to a dinner that made history in their small lives, and was eaten over again in happy dreams for months.

How those children did eat! And how beaming Miss Cornelia and grim-faced, soft-hearted Hannah and even the absent-minded teacher himself enjoyed watching them!

After dinner Miss Cornelia distributed among the delighted little souls the presents she had bought for them, and then turned them loose in the big shining kitchen to have a taffy pull—and they had it to their hearts' content! And as for the shocking, taffyfied state into which they got their own rosy faces and that once immaculate domain— well, as Miss Cornelia and Hannah never said one word about it, neither will I.

The four women enjoyed the afternoon in their own way, and the schoolteacher buried himself in algebra to his own great satisfaction.

When her guests went home in the starlit December dusk, Miss Cornelia walked part of the way with them and had a long confidential talk with Mrs. Grant. When she returned it was to find Hannah groaning in and over the kitchen and the schoolteacher dreamily trying to clean some molasses off his boots with the kitchen hairbrush. Long-suffering Miss Cornelia rescued her property and despatched Mr. Palmer into the woodshed to find the shoe-brush. Then she sat down and laughed.

"Hannah, what will become of that boy yet? There's no counting on what he'll do next. I don't know how he'll ever get through the world, I'm sure, but I'll look after him while he's here at least. I owe him a huge debt of gratitude for this Christmas blunder. What an awful mess this place is in! But, Hannah, did you ever in the world see anything so delightful as that little Tommy Smithson stuffing himself with plum cake, not to mention Teddy Grant? It did me good just to see them."

AUNT CYRILLA'S CHRISTMAS BASKET

When Lucy Rose met Aunt Cyrilla coming downstairs, somewhat flushed and breathless from her ascent to the garret, with a big, flat-covered basket hanging over her plump arm, she gave a little sigh of despair. Lucy Rose had done her brave best for some years—in fact, ever since she had put up her hair and lengthened her skirts—to break Aunt Cyrilla of the habit of carrying that basket with her every time she went to Pembroke; but Aunt Cyrilla still insisted on taking it, and only laughed at what she called Lucy Rose's "finicky notions." Lucy Rose had a horrible, haunting idea that it was extremely provincial for her aunt always to take the big basket, packed full of country good things, whenever she went to visit Edward and Geraldine. Geraldine was so stylish, and might think it queer; and then Aunt Cyrilla always would carry it on her arm and give cookies and apples and molasses taffy out of it to every child she encountered and, just as often as not, to older folks too. Lucy Rose, when she went to town with Aunt Cyrilla, felt chagrined over this—all of which goes to prove that Lucy was as yet very young and had a great deal to learn in this world.

That troublesome worry over what Geraldine would think nerved her to make a protest in this instance.

"Now, Aunt C'rilla," she pleaded, "you're surely not going to take that funny old basket to Pembroke this time—Christmas Day and all."

"'Deed and 'deed I am," returned Aunt Cyrilla briskly, as she put it on the table and proceeded to dust it out. "I never went to see Edward and Geraldine since they were married that I didn't take a basket of good things along with me for them, and I'm not going to stop now. As for it's being Christmas, all the more reason. Edward is always real glad to get some of the old farmhouse goodies. He says they beat city cooking all hollow, and so they do."

"But it's so countrified," moaned Lucy Rose.

"Well, I am countrified," said Aunt Cyrilla firmly, "and so are you. And what's more, I don't see that it's anything to be ashamed of. You've got some real silly pride about you, Lucy Rose. You'll grow out of it in time, but just now it is giving you a lot of trouble."

"The basket is a lot of trouble," said Lucy Rose crossly. "You're always mislaying it or afraid you will. And it does look so funny to be walking through the streets with that big, bulgy basket hanging on your arm."

"I'm not a mite worried about its looks," returned Aunt Cyrilla calmly. "As for its being a trouble, why, maybe it is, but I have that, and other people have the pleasure of it. Edward and Geraldine don't need it—I know that—but there may be those that will. And if it hurts your feelings to walk 'longside of a countrified old lady with a countrified basket, why, you can just fall behind, as it were."

Aunt Cyrilla nodded and smiled good-humouredly, and Lucy Rose, though she privately held to her own opinion, had to smile too.

"Now, let me see," said Aunt Cyrilla reflectively, tapping the snowy kitchen table with the point of her plump, dimpled forefinger, "what shall I take? That big fruit cake for one thing—Edward does like my fruit cake; and that cold boiled tongue for another. Those three mince pies too, they'd spoil before we got back or your uncle'd make himself sick eating them—mince pie is his besetting sin. And that little stone bottle full of cream—Geraldine may carry any amount of style, but I've yet to see her look down on real good country cream, Lucy Rose; and another bottle of my raspberry vinegar. That plate of jelly cookies and doughnuts will please the children and fill up the chinks, and you can bring me that box of ice-cream candy out of the pantry, and that bag of striped candy sticks your uncle brought home from the corner last night. And apples, of course—three or four dozen of those good eaters—and a little pot of my green-gage preserves—Edward'll like that. And some sandwiches and pound cake for a snack for ourselves. Now, I guess that will do for eatables. The presents for the children can go in on top. There's a doll for Daisy and the little boat your uncle made for Ray and a tatted lace handkerchief apiece for the twins, and the crochet hood for the baby. Now, is that all?"

"There's a cold roast chicken in the pantry," said Lucy Rose wickedly, "and the pig Uncle Leo killed is hanging up in the porch. Couldn't you put them in too?"

Aunt Cyrilla smiled broadly. "Well, I guess we'll leave the pig alone; but since you have reminded me of it, the chicken may as well go in. I can make room."

Lucy Rose, in spite of her prejudices, helped with the packing and, not having been trained under Aunt Cyrilla's eye for nothing, did it very well too, with much clever economy of space. But when Aunt Cyrilla had put in as a finishing touch a big bouquet of pink and white everlastings, and tied the bulging covers down with a firm hand, Lucy Rose stood over the basket and whispered vindictively:

"Some day I'm going to burn this basket—when I get courage enough. Then there'll be an end of lugging it everywhere we go like a—like an old market-woman."

Uncle Leopold came in just then, shaking his head dubiously. He was not going to spend Christmas with Edward and Geraldine, and perhaps the prospect of having to cook and eat his Christmas dinner all alone made him pessimistic.

"I mistrust you folks won't get to Pembroke tomorrow," he said sagely. "It's going to storm."

Aunt Cyrilla did not worry over this. She believed matters of this kind were fore-ordained, and she slept calmly. But Lucy Rose got up three times in the night to see if it were storming, and when she did sleep had horrible night-mares of struggling through blinding snowstorms dragging Aunt Cyrilla's Christmas basket along with her.

It was not snowing in the early morning, and Uncle Leopold drove Aunt Cyrilla and Lucy Rose and the basket to the station, four miles off. When they reached there the air was thick with flying flakes. The stationmaster sold them their tickets with a grim face.

"If there's any more snow comes, the trains might as well keep Christmas too," he said. "There's been so much snow already that traffic is blocked half the time, and now there ain't no place to shovel the snow off onto."

Aunt Cyrilla said that if the train were to get to Pembroke in time for Christmas, it would get there; and she opened her basket and gave the stationmaster and three small boys an apple apiece.

"That's the beginning," groaned Lucy Rose to herself.

When their train came along Aunt Cyrilla established herself in one seat and her basket in another, and looked beamingly around her at her fellow travellers.

These were few in number—a delicate little woman at the end of the car, with a baby and four other children, a young girl across the aisle with a pale, pretty face, a sun-burned lad three seats ahead in a khaki uniform, a very handsome, imposing old lady in a sealskin coat ahead of him, and a thin young man with spectacles opposite.

"A minister," reflected Aunt Cyrilla, beginning to clas-sify, "who takes better care of other folks' souls than of his own body; and that woman in the sealskin is discontented and cross at something—got up too early to catch the train, maybe; and that young chap must be one of the boys not long out of the hospital. That woman's children look as if they hadn't enjoyed a square meal since they were born; and if that girl across from me has a mother, I'd like to know what the woman means, letting her daughter go from home in this weather in clothes like that."

Lucy Rose merely wondered uncomfortably what the others thought of Aunt Cyrilla's basket.

They expected to reach Pembroke that night, but as the day wore on the storm grew worse. Twice the train had to stop while the train hands dug it out. The third time it could not go on. It was dusk when the conductor came through the train, replying brusquely to the questions of the anxious passengers.

"A nice lookout for Christmas—no, impossible to go on or back—track blocked for miles—what's that, madam?—no, no station near—woods for miles. We're here for the night. These storms of late have played the mischief with everything."

"Oh, dear," groaned Lucy Rose.

Aunt Cyrilla looked at her basket complacently. "At any rate, we won't starve," she said.

The pale, pretty girl seemed indifferent. The sealskin lady looked crosser than ever. The khaki boy said, "Just my luck," and two of the children began to cry. Aunt Cyrilla took some apples and striped candy sticks from her basket and carried them to them. She lifted the oldest into her ample lap and soon had them all around her, laughing and contented.

The rest of the travellers straggled over to the corner and drifted into conversation. The khaki boy said it was hard lines not to get home for Christmas, after all.

"I was invalided from South Africa three months ago, and I've been in the hospital at Netley ever since. Reached Halifax three days ago and telegraphed the old folks I'd eat my Christmas dinner with them, and to have an extra-big turkey because I didn't have any last year. They'll be badly disappointed."

He looked disappointed too. One khaki sleeve hung empty by his side. Aunt Cyrilla passed him an apple.

"We were all going down to Grandpa's for Christmas," said the little mother's oldest boy dolefully. "We've never been there before, and it's just too bad."

He looked as if he wanted to cry but thought better of it and bit off a mouthful of candy.

"Will there be any Santa Claus on the train?" demanded his small sister tearfully. "Jack says there won't."

"I guess he'll find you out," said Aunt Cyrilla reassuringly.

The pale, pretty girl came up and took the baby from the tired mother. "What a dear little fellow," she said softly.

"Are you going home for Christmas too?" asked Aunt Cyrilla.

The girl shook her head. "I haven't any home. I'm just a shop girl out of work at present, and I'm going to Pembroke to look for some."

Aunt Cyrilla went to her basket and took out her box of cream candy. "I guess we might as well enjoy ourselves. Let's eat it all up and have a good time. Maybe we'll get down to Pembroke in the morning."

The little group grew cheerful as they nibbled, and even the pale girl brightened up. The little mother told Aunt Cyrilla her story aside. She had been long estranged from her family, who had disapproved of her marriage. Her husband had died the previous summer, leaving her in poor circumstances.

"Father wrote to me last week and asked me to let bygones be bygones and come home for Christmas. I was so glad. And the children's hearts were set on it. It seems too bad that we are not to get there. I have to be back at work the morning after Christmas."

The khaki boy came up again and shared the candy. He told amusing stories of campaigning in South Africa. The minister came too, and listened, and even the sealskin lady turned her head over her shoulder.

By and by the children fell asleep, one on Aunt Cyrilla's lap and one on Lucy Rose's, and two on the seat. Aunt Cyrilla and the pale girl helped the mother make up beds for them. The minister gave his overcoat and the sealskin lady came forward with a shawl.

"This will do for the baby," she said.

"We must get up some Santa Claus for these young-sters," said the khaki boy. "Let's hang their stockings on the wall and fill 'em up as best we can. I've nothing about me but some hard cash and a jack-knife. I'll give each of 'em a quarter and the boy can have the knife."

"I've nothing but money either," said the sealskin lady regretfully.

Aunt Cyrilla glanced at the little mother. She had fallen asleep with her head against the seat-back.

"I've got a basket over there," said Aunt Cyrilla firmly, "and I've some presents in it that I was taking to my neph-ew's children. I'm going to give 'em to these. As for the money, I think the mother is the one for it to go to. She's been telling me her story, and a pitiful one it is. Let's make up a little purse among us for a Christmas present."

The idea met with favour. The khaki boy passed his cap and everybody contributed. The sealskin lady put in a crumpled note. When Aunt Cyrilla straightened it out she saw that it was for twenty dollars.

Meanwhile, Lucy Rose had brought the basket. She smiled at Aunt Cyrilla as she lugged it down the aisle and

Aunt Cyrilla smiled back. Lucy Rose had never touched that basket of her own accord before.

Ray's boat went to Jacky, and Daisy's doll to his oldest sister, the twins' lace handkerchiefs to the two smaller girls and the hood to the baby. Then the stockings were filled up with doughnuts and jelly cookies and the money was put in an envelope and pinned to the little mother's jacket.

"That baby is such a dear little fellow," said the sealskin lady gently. "He looks something like my little son. He died eighteen Christmases ago."

Aunt Cyrilla put her hand over the lady's kid glove. "So did mine," she said. Then the two women smiled tenderly at each other. Afterwards they rested from their labours and all had what Aunt Cyrilla called a "snack" of sandwiches and pound cake. The khaki boy said he hadn't tasted anything half so good since he left home.

"They didn't give us pound cake in South Africa," he said.

When morning came the storm was still raging. The children wakened and went wild with delight over their stockings. The little mother found her envelope and tried to utter thanks and broke down; and nobody knew what to say or do, when the conductor fortunately came in and made a diversion by telling them they might as well resign themselves to spending Christmas on the train.

"This is serious," said the khaki boy, "when you consider that we've no provisions. Don't mind for myself, used to half rations or no rations at all. But these kiddies will have tremendous appetites."

Then Aunt Cyrilla rose to the occasion.

"I've got some emergency rations here," she announced. "There's plenty for all and we'll have our Christmas dinner, although a cold one. Breakfast first thing. There's a sandwich apiece left and we must fill up on what is left of the cookies and doughnuts and save the rest for a real good spread at dinner time. The only thing is, I haven't any bread."

"I've a box of soda crackers," said the little mother eagerly.

Nobody in that car will ever forget that Christmas. To begin with, after breakfast they had a concert. The khaki boy gave two recitations, sang three songs, and gave a whistling solo. Lucy Rose gave three recitations and the minister a comic reading. The pale shop girl sang two songs. It was agreed that the khaki boy's whistling solo was the best number, and Aunt Cyrilla gave him the bouquet of everlastings as a reward of merit.

Then the conductor came in with the cheerful news that the storm was almost over and he thought the track would be cleared in a few hours.

"If we can get to the next station we'll be all right," he said. "The branch joins the main line there and the tracks will be clear."

At noon they had dinner. The train hands were invited in to share it. The minister carved the chicken with the brakeman's jack-knife and the khaki boy cut up the tongue and the mince pies, while the sealskin lady mixed the raspberry vinegar with its due proportion of water. Bits of paper served as plates. The train furnished a couple of glasses, a tin pint cup was discovered and given to the children, Aunt Cyrilla and Lucy Rose and the sealskin lady drank, turn about, from the latter's graduated medicine glass, the shop girl and the little mother shared one of the empty bottles, and the khaki boy, the minister, and the train men drank out of the other bottle.

Everybody declared they had never enjoyed a meal more in their lives. Certainly it was a merry one, and Aunt

Cyrilla's cooking was never more appreciated; indeed, the bones of the chicken and the pot of preserves were all that was left. They could not eat the preserves because they had no spoons, so Aunt Cyrilla gave them to the little mother.

When all was over, a hearty vote of thanks was passed to Aunt Cyrilla and her basket. The sealskin lady wanted to know how she made her pound cake, and the khaki boy asked for her receipt for jelly cookies. And when two hours later the conductor came in and said the snowploughs had got along and they'd soon be starting, they all wondered if it could really be less than twenty-four hours since they met.

"I feel as if I'd been campaigning with you all my life," said the khaki boy.

At the next station they all parted. The little mother and the children had to take the next train back home. The minister stayed there, and the khaki boy and the sealskin lady changed trains. The sealskin lady shook Aunt Cyrilla's hand. She no longer looked discontented or cross.

"This has been the pleasantest Christmas I have ever spent," she said heartily. "I shall never forget that wonderful basket of yours. The little shop girl is going home with me. I've promised her a place in my husband's store."

When Aunt Cyrilla and Lucy Rose reached Pembroke there was nobody to meet them because everyone had given up expecting them. It was not far from the station to Edward's house and Aunt Cyrilla elected to walk.

"I'll carry the basket," said Lucy Rose.

Aunt Cyrilla relinquished it with a smile. Lucy Rose smiled too.

"It's a blessed old basket," said the latter, "and I love it. Please forget all the silly things I ever said about it, Aunt C'rilla."

William Dean Howells

1837–1920

CHRISTMAS EVERY DAY

The little girl came into her papa's study, as she always did Saturday morning before breakfast, and asked for a story. He tried to beg off that morning, for he was very busy, but she would not let him. So he began:

"Well, once there was a little pig—"

She put her hand over his mouth and stopped him at the word. She said she had heard little pig stories till she was perfectly sick of them.

"Well, what kind of story *shall* I tell, then?"

"About Christmas. It's getting to be the season. It's past Thanksgiving already."

"It seems to me," argued her papa, "that I've told as often about Christmas as I have about little pigs."

"No difference! Christmas is more interesting."

"Well!" Her papa roused himself from his writing by a great effort. "Well, then, I'll tell you about the little girl that wanted it Christmas every day in the year. How would you like that?"

"First-rate!" said the little girl; and she nestled into comfortable shape in his lap, ready for listening.

"Very well, then, this little pig,—Oh, what are you pounding me for?"

"Because you said little pig instead of little girl."

"I should like to know what's the difference between a little pig and a little girl that wanted it Christmas every day!"

"Papa!" said the little girl, warningly, "if you don't go on, I'll *give* it to you!" And at this her papa darted off like lightning, and began to tell the story as fast as he could.

Well, once there was a little girl who liked Christmas so much that she wanted it to be Christmas every day in the year; and as soon as Thanksgiving was over she began to send postal cards to the old Christmas Fairy to ask if she mightn't have it. But the old Fairy never answered any of the postals; and, after a while, the little girl found out that the Fairy was pretty particular, and wouldn't notice anything but letters, not even correspondence cards in envelopes; but real letters on sheets of paper, and sealed outside with a monogram,—or your initial, anyway. So, then, she began to send her letters; and in about three weeks—or just the day before Christmas, it was—she got a letter from the Fairy, saying she might have it Christmas every day for a year, and then they would see about having it longer.

The little girl was a good deal excited already, preparing for the old-fashioned, once-a-year Christmas that was coming the next day, and perhaps the Fairy's promise didn't make such an impression on her as it would have made at some other time. She just resolved to keep it to herself, and surprise everybody with it as it kept coming true; and then it slipped out of her mind altogether.

She had a splendid Christmas. She went to bed early, so as to let Santa Claus have a chance at the stockings, and in the morning she was up the first of anybody and went and felt them, and found hers all lumpy with packages of candy, and oranges and grapes, and pocket-books and rubber balls and all kinds of small presents, and her big brother's with nothing but the tongs in them, and her young lady sister's with a new silk umbrella, and her papa's and mamma's with potatoes and pieces of coal wrapped up in tissue paper, just as they always had every Christmas. Then she waited around till the rest of the family were up, and she was the first to burst into the library, when the doors were opened, and look at the large presents laid out on the library-table—books, and portfolios, and boxes of stationery, and breast-pins, and dolls, and little stoves, and dozens of handkerchiefs, and ink-stands, and skates, and snow-shovels, and photograph-frames, and little easels, and boxes of water-colors, and Turkish paste, and nougat, and candied cherries, and dolls' houses, and waterproofs,—and the big Christmas-tree, lighted and standing in a waste-basket in the middle.

She had a splendid Christmas all day. She ate so much candy that she did not want any breakfast; and the whole forenoon the presents kept pouring in that the expressman had not had to deliver the night before; and she went 'round giving the presents she had got for other people and came home and ate turkey and cranberry dinner, and plum-pudding and nuts and raisins and oranges and more candy, and then went home and coasted and came in with a stomache-ache, crying, and her papa said he would see if his house was turned into that sort of fool's paradise another year, and they had a light supper, and pretty early everybody went to bed cross.

Here the little girl pounded her papa in the back, again.

"Well, what now? Did I say pigs?"

"You made them *act* like pigs."

"Well, didn't they?"

"No matter; you oughtn't to put it into a story."

"Very well, then, I'll take it all out."

Her father went on:

The little girl slept very heavily, and she very late, but she was wakened at last by the other children dancing 'round her bed with their stockings full of presents in their hands.

"What is it?" said the little girl, and she rubbed her eyes and tried to rise up in bed.

"Christmas! Christmas! Christmas!" they all shouted, and waved their stockings.

"Nonsense! It was Christmas yesterday."

Her brothers and sisters just laughed. "We don't know about that. It's Christmas to-day, anyway. You come into the library and see."

Then all at once it flashed on the little girl that the Fairy was keeping her promise, and her year of Christmases was beginning. She was dreadfully sleepy, but she sprang up like a lark—a lark that had overeaten itself and gone to bed cross—and darted into the library. There it was again! Books and portfolios, and boxes of stationery, and breast-pins—

"You needn't go over it all, Papa; I guess I can remember just what was there," said the little girl.

Well, and there was the Christmas-tree blazing away, and the family picking out their presents, but looking pretty sleepy, and her father perfectly puzzled, and her mother ready to cry. "I'm sure I don't see how I'm to dispose of all these things," said her mother, and her father said it seemed to him they had had something just like it the day before, but he supposed he must have dreamed it. This struck the little girl as the best kind of a joke; and so she ate so much candy she didn't want any breakfast, and went 'round carrying presents, and had turkey and cranberry for dinner, and then went out and coasted, and came in with a—

"Papa!"
"Well, what now?"
"What did you promise, you forgetful thing?"
"Oh! oh, yes!"

Well, the next day, it was just the same thing over again, but everybody getting crosser; and at the end of a week's time so many people had lost their tempers that you could pick up lost tempers anywhere; they perfectly strewed the ground. Even when people tried to recover their tempers they usually got somebody else's, and it made the most dreadful mix.

The little girl began to get frightened, keeping the secret all to herself; she wanted to tell her mother, but she didn't dare to; and she was ashamed to ask the Fairy to take back her gift, it seemed ungrateful and ill-bred, and she thought she would try to stand it, but she hardly knew how she could, for a whole year. So it went on and on, and it was Christmas on St. Valentine's Day, and Washington's Birthday, just the same as any day, and it didn't skip even the First of April, though everything was counterfeit that day, and that was some *little* relief.

After a while, coal and potatoes began to be awfully scarce, so many had been wrapped up in tissue paper to fool papas and mammas with. Turkeys got to be about a thousand dollars apiece—

"Papa!"
"Well, what?"

151

"You're beginning to fib."

"Well, *two* thousand, then."

And they got to passing off almost anything for turkeys,—half-grown humming-birds, and even rocs out of the *Arabian Nights,*—the real turkeys were so scarce. And cranberries—well, they asked a diamond apiece for cranberries. All the woods and orchards were cut down for Christmas-trees, and where the woods and orchards used to be, it looked just like a stubble-field, with the stumps. After a while they had to make Christmas-trees out of rags, and stuff them with bran, like old-fashioned dolls; but there were plenty of rags, because people got so poor, buying presents for one another, that they couldn't get any new clothes, and they just wore their old ones to tatters. They got so poor that everybody had to go to the poorhouse, except the confectioners, and the fancy store-keepers, and the picture-booksellers, and the expressmen; and *they* all got so rich and proud that they would hardly wait upon a person when he came to buy; it was perfectly shameful!

Well, after it had gone on about three or four months, the little girl, whenever she came into the room in the morning and saw those great ugly lumpy stockings dangling at the fire-place, and the disgusting presents around everywhere, used to just sit down and burst out crying. In six months she was perfectly exhausted; she couldn't even cry any more; she just lay on the lounge and rolled her eyes and panted. About the beginning of October she took to sitting down on dolls, wherever she found them,—French dolls, or any kind,—she hated the sight of them so; and by Thanksgiving she was crazy, and just slammed her presents across the room.

By that time people didn't carry presents around nicely any more. They flung them over the fence, or through the window, or anything; and, instead of running their tongues out and taking great pains to write "For dear Papa," or "Mamma," or "Brother," or "Sister," or "Susie," or "Sammie," or "Billie," or "Bobby," or "Jimmie," or "Jennie," or whoever it was, and troubling to get the spelling right, and then signing their names, and "'Xmas, 188—,'" they used to write in the gift-books, "Take it, you horrid old thing!" and then go and bang it against the front door. Nearly everybody had built barns to hold their presents, but pretty soon the barns overflowed, and then they used to let them lie out in the rain, or anywhere. Sometimes the police used to come and tell them to shovel their presents off the sidewalk, or they would arrest them.

"I thought you said everybody had gone to the poor-house," interrupted the little girl.

"They did go, at first," said her papa; "but after a while the poor-houses got so full that they had to send the people back to their own houses. They tried to cry, when they got back, but they couldn't make the least sound."

"Why couldn't they?"

"Because they had lost their voices, saying 'Merry Christmas' so much. Did I tell you how it was on the Fourth of July?"

"No; how was it?" And the little girl nestled closer, in expectation of something uncommon.

Well, the night before, the boys stayed up to celebrate, as they always do, and fell asleep before twelve o'clock, as usual, expecting to be awakened by the bells and cannon. But it was nearly eight o'clock before the first boy in the United States woke up, and then he found out what the trouble was. As soon as he could get his clothes on, he ran out of the house and smashed a big cannon-torpedo down on the pavement; but it didn't make any more noise than a damp wad of paper, and, after he tried about twenty or thirty more, he began to pick them up and look at them. Every single torpedo was a big raisin! Then he just streaked it upstairs, and examined his fire-crackers and toy-pistol and two-dollar collection of fireworks, and found that they were nothing but sugar and candy painted up to look like fireworks! Before ten o'clock, every boy in the United States found out that his Fourth of July things had turned into Christmas things; and then they just sat down and cried,—they were so mad. There are about twenty million boys in the United States, and so you can imagine what a noise they made. Some men got together before night, with a little powder that hadn't turned into purple sugar yet, and they said they would fire off *one* cannon, anyway. But the cannon burst into a thousand pieces, for it was nothing but rock-candy, and some of the men nearly got killed. The Fourth of July orations all turned into Christmas carols, and when anybody tried to read the Declaration, instead of saying, "When in the course of human events it becomes necessary," he was sure to sing, "God rest you, merry gentlemen." It was perfectly awful.

The little girl drew a deep sigh of satisfaction. "And how was it at Thanksgiving?" she asked.

Her papa hesitated. "Well, I'm almost afraid to tell you. I'm afraid you'll think it's wicked."

"Well, tell, anyway," said the little girl.

Well, before it came Thanksgiving, it had leaked out who had caused all these Christmases. The little girl had suffered so much that she had talked about it in her sleep; and after that, hardly anybody would play with her. People just perfectly despised her, because if it had not been for her greediness, it wouldn't have happened; and now, when it came Thanksgiving, and she wanted them to go to church, and have squash-pie and turkey, and show their gratitude, they said that all the turkeys had been eaten for her old Christmas dinners, and if she would stop the Christmases, they would see about the gratitude. Wasn't it dreadful? And the very next day the little girl began to send letters to the Christmas Fairy, and then telegrams, to stop it. But it didn't do any good; and then she got to calling at the Fairy's house, but the girl that came to the door always said, "Not at home," or "Engaged," or "At dinner," or something like that; and so it went on till it came to the old once-a-year Christmas Eve. The little girl fell asleep, and when she woke up in the morning—

"She found it was all nothing but a dream," suggested the little girl.

"No indeed!" said her papa. "It was all every bit true!"

"Well, what *did* she find out, then?"

"Why, that it wasn't Christmas at last, and wasn't ever going to be, any more. Now it's time for breakfast."

The little girl held her papa fast around the neck.

"You sha'n't go if you're going to leave it *so*!"

"How do you want it left?"

"Christmas once a year."

"All right," said her papa, and he went on again.

Well, there was the greatest rejoicing all over the country, and it extended clear up into Canada. The people met together everywhere, and kissed and cried for joy. The city carts went around and gathered up all the candy and raisins and nuts, and dumped them into the river; and it made the fish perfectly sick; and the whole United States, as far out as Alaska, was one blaze of bonfires, where the children were burning up their gift-books and presents of all kinds. They had the greatest *time*!

The little girl went to thank the old Fairy because she had stopped its being Christmas, and she said she hoped she would keep her promise, and see that Christmas never, never came again. Then the Fairy frowned, and asked her if she was sure she knew what she meant; and the little girl asked her, why not? and the old Fairy said that now she was behaving just as greedily as ever, and she'd better look out. This made the little girl think it all over carefully again, and she said she would be willing to have it Christmas about once in a thousand years; and then she said a hundred, and then she said ten, and at last she got down to one. Then the Fairy said that was the good old way that had pleased people ever since Christmas began, and she was agreed. Then the little girl said, "What're your shoes made of?" And the Fairy said, "Leather." And the little girl said, "Bargain's done forever," and skipped off, and hippity-hopped the whole way home, she was so glad.

"How will that do?" asked the papa.

"First-rate!" said the little girl; but she hated to have the story stop, and was rather sober. However, her mamma put her head in at the door, and asked her papa:

"Are you never coming to breakfast? What have you been telling that child?"

"Oh, just a moral tale."

The little girl caught him around the neck again.

"*We* know! Don't you tell *what*, Papa! Don't you tell *what!*"

Harriet Beecher Stowe

1811–1896

CHRISTMAS; OR, THE GOOD FAIRY

"O, dear! Christmas is coming in a fortnight, and I have got to think up presents for every body!" said young Ellen Stuart, as she leaned languidly back in her chair. "Dear me, it's so tedious! Every body has got every thing that can be thought of."

"O, no," said her confidential adviser, Miss Lester, in a soothing tone. "You have means of buying every thing you can fancy; and when every shop and store is glittering with all manner of splendors, you cannot surely be at a loss."

"Well, now, just listen. To begin with, there's mamma. What can I get for her? I have thought of ever so many things. She has three card cases, four gold thimbles, two or three gold chains, two writing desks of different patterns; and then as to rings, brooches, boxes, and all other things, I should think she might be sick of the sight of them. I am sure I am," said she, languidly gazing on her white and jewelled fingers.

This view of the case seemed rather puzzling to the adviser, and there was silence for a few moments, when Ellen, yawning, resumed:—

"And then there's Cousins Jane and Mary; I suppose they will be coming down on me with a whole load of presents; and Mrs. B. will send me something—she did last year; and then there's Cousins William and Tom—I must get them something; and I would like to do it well enough, if I only knew what to get."

"Well," said Eleanor's aunt, who had been sitting quietly rattling her knitting needles during this speech, "it's a pity that you had not such a subject to practise on as I was when I was a girl. Presents did not fly about in those days as they do now. I remember, when I was ten years old, my father gave me a most marvellously ugly sugar dog for a Christmas gift, and I was perfectly delighted with it, the very idea of a present was so new to us."

"Dear aunt, how delighted I should be if I had any such fresh, unsophisticated body to get presents for! But to get and get for people that have more than they know what to do with now; to add pictures, books, and gilding when the centre tables are loaded with them now, and rings and jewels when they are a perfect drug! I wish myself that I were not sick, and sated, and tired with having every thing in the world given me."

"Well, Eleanor," said her aunt, "if you really do want unsophisticated subjects to practise on, I can put you in the way of it. I can show you more than one family to whom you might seem to be a very good fairy, and where such gifts as you could give with all ease would seem like a magic dream."

"Why, that would really be worth while, aunt."

"Look over in that back alley," said her aunt. "You see those buildings?"

"That miserable row of shanties? Yes."

"Well, I have several acquaintances there who have never been tired of Christmas gifts, or gifts of any other kind. I assure you, you could make quite a sensation over there."

"Well, who is there? Let us know."

"Do you remember Owen, that used to make your shoes?"

"Yes, I remember something about him."

"Well, he has fallen into a consumption, and cannot work any more; and he, and his wife, and three little children live in one of the rooms."

"How do they get along?"

"His wife takes in sewing sometimes, and sometimes goes out washing. Poor Owen! I was over there yesterday; he looks thin and wasted, and his wife was saying that he was parched with constant fever, and had very little appetite. She had, with great self-denial, and by restricting herself almost of necessary food, got him two or three oranges; and the poor fellow seemed so eager after them!"

"Poor fellow!" said Eleanor, involuntarily.

"Now," said her aunt, "suppose Owen's wife should get up on Christmas morning and find at the door a couple of dozen of oranges, and some of those nice white grapes, such as you had at your party last week; don't you think it would make a sensation?"

"Why, yes, I think very likely it might; but who else, aunt? You spoke of a great many."

"Well, on the lower floor there is a neat little room, that is always kept perfectly trim and tidy; it belongs to a young couple who have nothing beyond the husband's day wages to live on. They are, nevertheless, as cheerful and chipper as a couple of wrens; and she is up and down half a dozen times a day, to help poor Mrs. Owen. She has a baby of her own, about five months old, and of course does all the cooking, washing, and ironing for herself and husband; and yet, when Mrs. Owen goes out to wash, she takes her baby, and keeps it whole days for her."

"I'm sure she deserves that the good fairies should smile on her," said Eleanor; "one baby exhausts my stock of virtues very rapidly."

"But you ought to see her baby," said Aunt E.; "so plump, so rosy, and good-natured, and always clean as a lily. This baby is a sort of household shrine; nothing is too sacred or too good for it; and I believe the little thrifty woman feels only one temptation to be extravagant, and that is to get some ornaments to adorn this little divinity."

"Why, did she ever tell you so?"

"No; but one day, when I was coming down stairs, the door of their room was partly open, and I saw a peddler there with open box. John, the husband, was standing with a little purple cap on his hand, which he was regarding with mystified, admiring air, as if he didn't quite comprehend it, and trim little Mary gazing at it with longing eyes.

"'I think we might get it,' said John.

"'O, no,' said she, regretfully; 'yet I wish we could, it's *so pretty!*'"

"Say no more, aunt. I see the good fairy must pop a cap into the window on Christmas morning. Indeed, it shall be done. How they will wonder where it came from, and talk about it for months to come!"

"Well, then," continued her aunt, "in the next street to ours there is a miserable building, that looks as if it were just going to topple over; and away up in the third story, in a little room just under the eaves, live two poor, lonely old women. They are both nearly on to ninety. I was in there day before yesterday. One of them is constantly confined to her bed with rheumatism; the other, weak and feeble, with failing sight and trembling hands, totters about, her only helper; and they are entirely dependent on charity."

"Can't they do any thing? Can't they knit?" said Eleanor.

"You are young and strong, Eleanor, and have quick

eyes and nimble fingers; how long would it take you to knit a pair of stockings?"

"I?" said Eleanor. "What an idea! I never tried, but I think I could get a pair done in a week, perhaps."

"And if somebody gave you twenty-five cents for them, and out of this you had to get food, and pay room rent, and buy coal for your fire, and oil for your lamp—"

"Stop, aunt, for pity's sake!"

"Well, I will stop; but they can't: they must pay so much every month for that miserable shell they live in, or be turned into the street. The meal and flour that some kind person sends goes off for them just as it does for others, and they must get more or starve; and coal is now scarce and high priced."

"O aunt, I'm quite convinced, I'm sure; don't run me down and annihilate me with all these terrible realities. What shall I do to play good fairy to these poor old women?"

"If you will give me full power, Eleanor, I will put up a basket to be sent to them that will give them something to remember all winter."

"O, certainly I will. Let me see if I can't think of something myself."

"Well, Eleanor, suppose, then, some fifty or sixty years hence, *if* you were old, and your father, and mother, and aunts, and uncles, now so thick around you, lay cold and silent in so many graves—you have somehow got away off to a strange city, where you were never known—you live in a miserable garret, where snow blows at night through the cracks, and the fire is very apt to go out in the old cracked stove—you sit crouching over the dying embers the evening before Christmas—nobody to speak to you, nobody to care for you, except another poor old soul who lies moaning in the bed. Now, what would you like to have sent you?"

"O aunt, what a dismal picture!"

"And yet, Ella, all poor, forsaken old women are made of young girls, who expected it in their youth as little as you do, perhaps."

"Say no more, aunt. I'll buy—let me see—a comfortable warm shawl for each of these poor women; and I'll send them—let me see—O, some tea—nothing goes down with old women like tea; and I'll make John wheel some coal over to them; and, aunt, it would not be a very bad thought to send them a new stove. I remember, the other day, when mamma was pricing stoves, I saw some such nice ones for two or three dollars."

"For a new hand, Ella, you work up the idea very well," said her aunt.

"But how much ought I to give, for any one case, to these women, say?"

"How much did you give last year for any single Christmas present?"

"Why, six or seven dollars for some; those elegant souvenirs were seven dollars; that ring I gave Mrs. B. was twenty."

"And do you suppose Mrs. B. was any happier for it?"

"No, really, I don't think she cared much about it; but I had to give her something, because she had sent me something the year before, and I did not want to send a paltry present to one in her circumstances."

"Then, Ella, give the same to any poor, distressed, suffering creature who really needs it, and see in how many forms of good such a sum will appear. That one hard, cold, glittering ring, that now cheers nobody, and means nothing, that you give because you must, and she takes because she must, might, if broken up into smaller sums, send real warm and heartfelt gladness through many a cold and cheerless dwelling, through many an aching heart."

"You are getting to be an orator, aunt; but don't you approve of Christmas presents, among friends and equals?"

"Yes, indeed," said her aunt, fondly stroking her head. "I have had some Christmas presents that did me a world of good—a little book mark, for instance, that a certain niece of mine worked for me, with wonderful secrecy, three years ago, when she was not a young lady with a purse full of money—that book mark was a true Christmas present; and my young couple across the way are plotting a profound surprise to each other on Christmas morning. John has contrived, by an hour of extra work every night, to lay by enough to get Mary a new calico dress; and she, poor soul, has bargained away the only thing in the jewelry line she ever possessed, to be laid out on a new hat for him.

"I know, too, a washerwoman who has a poor, lame boy—a patient, gentle little fellow—who has lain quietly for weeks and months in his little crib, and his mother is going to give him a splendid Christmas present."

"What is it, pray?"

"A whole orange! Don't laugh. She will pay ten whole

cents for it; for it shall be none of your common oranges, but a picked one of the very best going! She has put by the money, a cent at a time, for a whole month; and nobody knows which will be happiest in it, Willie or his mother. These are such Christmas presents as I like to think of— gifts coming from love, and tending to produce love; these are the appropriate gifts of the day."

"But don't you think that it's right for those who *have* money to give expensive presents, supposing always, as you say, they are given from real affection?"

"Sometimes, undoubtedly. The Savior did not condemn her who broke an alabaster box of ointment—*very precious*—simply as a proof of love, even although the suggestion was made, 'This might have been sold for three hundred pence, and given to the poor.' I have thought he would regard with sympathy the fond efforts which human love sometimes makes to express itself by gifts, the rarest and most costly. How I rejoiced with all my heart, when Charles Elton gave his poor mother that splendid Chinese shawl and gold watch! because I knew they came from the very fulness of his heart to a mother that he could not do too much for—a mother that has done and suffered every thing for him. In some such cases, when resources are ample, a costly gift seems to have a graceful appropriateness; but I cannot approve of it if it exhausts all the means of doing for the poor; it is better, then, to give a simple offering, and to do something for those who really need it."

Eleanor looked thoughtful; her aunt laid down her knitting, and said, in a tone of gentle seriousness, "Whose birth does Christmas commemorate, Ella?"

"Our Savior's, certainly, aunt."

"Yes," said her aunt. "And when and how was he born? In a stable! laid in a manger; thus born, that in all ages he might be known as the brother and friend of the poor. And surely, it seems but appropriate to commemorate his birthday by an especial remembrance of the lowly, the poor, the outcast, and distressed; and if Christ should come back to our city on a Christmas day, where should we think it most appropriate to his character to find him? Would he be carrying splendid gifts to splendid dwellings, or would he be gliding about in the cheerless haunts of the desolate, the poor, the forsaken, and the sorrowful?"

And here the conversation ended.

"What sort of Christmas presents is Ella buying?" said Cousin Tom, as the waiter handed in a portentous-looking package, which had been just rung in at the door.

"Let's open it," said saucy Will. "Upon my word, two great gray blanket shawls! These must be for you and me, Tom! And what's this? A great bolt of cotton flannel and gray yarn stockings!"

The door bell rang again, and the waiter brought in another bulky parcel, and deposited it on the marble-topped centre table.

"What's here?" said Will, cutting the cord. "Whew! a perfect nest of packages! oolong tea! oranges! grapes! white sugar! Bless me, Ella must be going to housekeeping!"

"Or going crazy!" said Tom; "and on my word," said he, looking out of the window, "there's a drayman ringing at our door, with a stove, with a teakettle set in the top of it!"

"Ella's cook stove, of course," said Will; and just at this moment the young lady entered, with her purse hanging gracefully over her hand.

"Now, boys, you are too bad!" she exclaimed, as each of

the mischievous youngsters were gravely marching up and down, attired in a gray shawl.

"Didn't you get them for us? We thought you did," said both.

"Ella, I want some of that cotton flannel, to make me a pair of pantaloons," said Tom.

"I say, Ella," said Will, "when are you going to house-keeping? Your cooking stove is standing down in the street; 'pon my word, John is loading some coal on the dray with it."

"Ella, isn't that going to be sent to my office?" said Tom; "do you know I do so languish for a new stove with a teakettle in the top, to heat a fellow's shaving water!"

Just then, another ring at the door, and the grinning waiter handed in a small brown paper parcel for Miss Ella. Tom made a dive at it, and staving off the brown paper, developed a jaunty little purple velvet cap, with silver tassels.

"My smoking cap, as I live!" said he; "only I shall have to wear it on my thumb, instead of my head—too small entirely," said he, shaking his head gravely.

"Come, you saucy boys," said Aunt E., entering briskly, "what are you teasing Ella for?"

"Why, do see this lot of things, aunt! What in the world is Ella going to do with them?"

"O, I know!"

"You know! Then I can guess, aunt, it is some of your charitable works. You are going to make a juvenile Lady Bountiful of El, eh?"

Ella, who had colored to the roots of her hair at the *exposé* of her very unfashionable Christmas preparations, now took heart, and bestowed a very gentle and salutary little cuff on the saucy head that still wore the purple cap, and then hastened to gather up her various purchases.

"Laugh away," said she, gayly; "and a good many others will laugh, too, over these things. I got them to make people laugh—people that are not in the habit of laughing!"

"Well, well, I see into it," said Will; "and I tell you I think right well of the idea, too. There are worlds of money wasted, at this time of the year, in getting things that nobody wants, and nobody cares for after they are got; and I am glad, for my part, that you are going to get up a variety in this line; in fact, I should like to give you one of these stray leaves to help on," said he, dropping a ten dollar note into her paper. "I like to encourage girls to think of something besides breastpins and sugar candy."

But our story spins on too long. If any body wants to see the results of Ella's first attempts at *good fairyism*, they can call at the doors of two or three old buildings on Christmas morning, and they shall hear all about it.

CHRISTMAS IN POGANUC

The First Christmas

Can any of us look back to the earlier days of our mortal pilgrimage and remember the helpless sense of desolation and loneliness caused by being forced to go off to the stillness and darkness of a solitary bed far from all the beloved voices and employments and sights of life? Can we remember lying, hearing distant voices, and laughs of more fortunate, older people and the opening and shutting of distant doors, that told of scenes of animation and interest from which we were excluded? How doleful sounded the tick of the clock, and how dismal was the darkness as sunshine faded from the window, leaving only a square of dusky dimness in place of daylight!

All who remember these will sympathize with Dolly, who was hustled off to bed by Nabby the minute supper was over, that she might have the decks clear for action.

"Now be a good girl; shut your eyes, and say your prayers, and go right to sleep," had been Nabby's parting injunction as she went out, closing the door after her.

The little head sunk into the pillow, and Dolly recited her usual liturgy of "Our Father who art in heaven," and "I pray God to bless my dear father and mother and all my dear friends and relations, and make me a good girl," and ending with,

"'Now I lay me down to sleep.'"

But sleep she could not. The wide, bright, wistful blue eyes lay shining like two stars toward the fading light in the window, and the little ears were strained to catch every sound. She heard the shouts of Tom and Bill and the loud barking of Spring as they swept out of the door; and the sound went to her heart. Spring—her faithful attendant, the most loving and sympathetic of dogs, her friend and confidential counselor in many a solitary ramble—Spring had gone with the boys to see the sight, and left her alone. She began to pity herself and cry softly on her pillow. For a while she could hear Nabby's energetic movements below, washing up dishes, putting back chairs, and giving energetic thumps and bangs here and there, as her way was of producing order. But by and by that was all over, and she heard the loud shutting of the kitchen door and Nabby's voice chatting with her attendant as she went off to the scene of gaiety.

In those simple, innocent days in New England villages nobody thought of locking house doors at night. There was in those times no idea either of tramps or burglars, and many a night in summer had Dolly lain awake and heard the voices of tree-toads and whip-poor-wills mingling with the whisper of leaves and the swaying of elm boughs, while the great outside door of the house lay broad open in the moonlight. But then this was when everybody was in the house and asleep, when the door of her parents' room stood open on the front hall, and she knew she could run to the paternal bed in a minute for protection. Now, however, she knew the house was empty. Everybody had gone out of it; and there is something fearful to a little lonely body in the possibilities of a great, empty house. She got up and opened her door, and the "tick-tock" of the old kitchen clock for a moment seemed like company; but pretty soon its ticking began to strike louder and louder with a nervous insistency on her ear, till the nerves quivered and vibrated, and she couldn't go to sleep. She lay and listened to all the noises outside. It was a still, clear, freezing night, when the least sound clinked with a metallic resonance. She heard the runners of sleighs squeaking and crunching over the frozen road, and the lively jingle of bells. They would come nearer, nearer, pass by the house, and go off in the distance. Those were the happy folks going to see the gold star and the Christmas greens in the church. The gold star, the Christmas greens, had all the more attraction from their vagueness. Dolly was a fanciful little creature, and the clear air and romantic scenery of a mountain town had fed her imagination. Stories she had never read, except in the Bible and the *Pilgrim's Progress*, but her very soul had vibrated with the descriptions of the celestial city—something vague, bright, glorious, lying beyond some dark river; and Nabby's rude account of what was going on in the church suggested those images.

Finally a bright thought popped into her little head. She could see the church from the front windows of the house; she would go there and look. In haste she sprang out of bed and dressed herself. It was sharp and freezing in the fireless chamber, but Dolly's blood had a racing, healthy tingle to it; she didn't mind cold. She wrapped her cloak around her and tied on her hood and ran to the front windows. There it was, to be sure—the little church with its sharp-pointed windows, every pane of which was sending streams of light across the glittering snow. There was a crowd around the door, and men and boys looking in at the windows. Dolly's soul was fired. But the elm boughs a little obstructed her vision; she thought she would go down and look at it from the yard. So down-stairs she ran, but as she opened the door the sound of the chant rolled out into the darkness with sweet and solemn cadence:

"Glory be to God on high; and on earth peace, good will toward men."

Dolly's soul was all aglow—her nerves tingled and vibrated; she thought of the bells ringing in the celestial city; she could no longer contain herself, but faster and faster the little hooded form scudded across the snowy plain and pushed in among the dark cluster of spectators at the door. All made way for the child, and in a moment, whether in the body or out she could not tell, Dolly was sitting in a little nook under a bower of spruce, gazing at the star and listening to the voices:

"We praise Thee, we bless Thee, we worship Thee, we glorify Thee, we give thanks to Thee for Thy great glory, O Lord God, Heavenly King, God, the Father Almighty."

Her heart throbbed and beat; she trembled with a strange happiness and sat as one entranced till the music was over. Then came reading, the rustle and murmur of people kneeling, and then they all rose and there was the solemn buzz of voices repeating the Creed with a curious lulling sound to her ear. There was old Mr. Danforth with his spectacles on, reading with a pompous tone, as if to witness a good confession for the church; and there were Squire Lewis and old Ma'am Lewis; and there was one place where they all bowed their heads and all the ladies made courtesies—all of which entertained her mightily.

When the sermon began Dolly got fast asleep, and slept as quietly as a pet lamb in a meadow, lying in a little warm roll back under the shadows of the spruces. She was so tired and so sound asleep that she did not wake when the service ended, lying serenely curled up, and having perhaps pleas-ant dreams. She might have had the fortunes of little Goody

Two-Shoes, whose history was detailed in one of the few children's books then printed, had not two friends united to find her out.

Spring, who had got into the slip with the boys, and been an equally attentive and edified listener, after service began a tour of investigation, dog-fashion, with his nose; for how could a minister's dog form a suitable judgment of any new procedure if he was repressed from the use of his own leading faculty? So, Spring went round the church conscientiously, smelling at pew doors, smelling of the greens, smelling at the heels of gentlemen and ladies, till he came near the door of the church, when he suddenly smelt something which called for immediate attention, and he made a side dart into the thicket where Dolly was sleeping, and began licking her face and hands and pulling her dress, giving short barks occasionally, as if to say, "Come, Dolly, wake up!" At the same instant Hiel, who had seen her from the gallery, came down just as the little one was sitting up with a dazed, bewildered air.

"Why, Dolly, how came you out o' bed this time o' night? Don't ye know the nine o'clock bell's jest rung?"

Dolly knew Hiel well enough—what child in the village

did not? She reached up her little hands, saying in an apologetic fashion:

"They were all gone away, and I was so lonesome!"

Hiel took her up in his long arms and carried her home, and was just entering the house door with her as the sleigh drove up with Parson Cushing and his wife.

"Wal, Parson, your folks has all ben to the 'lumination—Nabby and Bill and Tom and Dolly here; found her all rolled up in a heap like a rabbit under the cedars."

"Why, Dolly Cushing!" exclaimed her mother. "What upon earth got you out of bed this time of night? You'll catch your death o' cold."

"I was all alone," said Dolly, with a piteous bleat.

"Oh, there, there, wife; don't say a word," put in the parson. "Get her off to bed. Never mind, Dolly, don't you cry"; for Parson Cushing was a soft-hearted gentleman and couldn't bear the sight of Dolly's quivering under lip. So Dolly told her little story, how she had been promised a sugar dog by Nabby if she'd be a good girl and go to sleep, and how she couldn't go to sleep, and how she just went down to look from the yard, and how the music drew her right over.

"There, there," said Parson Cushing, "go to bed, Dolly; and if Nabby don't give you a sugar dog, I will. This Christmas dressing is all nonsense," he added, "but the child's not to blame—it was natural."

"After all," he said to his wife the last thing after they were settled for the night, "our little Dolly is an unusual child. There were not many little girls that would have dared to do that. I shall preach a sermon right away that will set all this Christmas matter straight," said the Doctor. "There is not a shadow of evidence that the first Christians kept Christmas. It wasn't kept for the first three centuries, nor was Christ born anywhere near the 25th of December."

The next morning found little Dolly's blue eyes wide open with all the wondering eagerness of a new idea.

Dolly had her wise thoughts about Christmas. She had been terribly frightened at first, when she was brought home from the church; but when her papa kissed her and promised her a sugar dog she was quite sure that, whatever the unexplained mystery might be, he did not think the lovely scene of the night before a wicked one. And when Mrs. Cushing came and covered the little girl up warmly in bed, she only said to her, "Dolly, you must never get out of bed again at night after you are put there; you might have caught a dreadful cold and been sick and died, and then we should have lost our little Dolly." So Dolly promised quite readily to be good and lie still ever after, no matter what attractions might be on foot in the community.

Much was gained, however, and it was all clear gain; and forthwith the little fanciful head proceeded to make the most of it, thinking over every feature of the wonder. The child had a vibrating, musical organization, and the sway and rush of the chanting still sounded in her ears and reminded her of that wonderful story in the *Pilgrim's Progress*, where the gate of the celestial city swung open, and there were voices that sung, "Blessing and honor and glory and power be unto Him who sitteth on the throne." And then that wonderful star, that shone just as if it were a real star—how could it be! For Miss Ida Lewis, being a young lady of native artistic genius, had cut a little hole in the centre of her gilt paper star, behind which was placed a candle, so that it gave real light, in a way most astonishing to untaught eyes. In Dolly's simple view it verged on the supernatural—perhaps it was *the* very real star read about in the Gospel story. Why not? Dolly was at the happy age when anything bright and heavenly seemed credible, and had the child-faith to which all things were possible.

"I wish, my dear," said Mrs. Cushing, after they were retired to their room for the night, "that to-morrow morning you would read the account of the birth of Christ in St. Matthew, and give the children some advice upon the proper way of keeping Christmas."

"Well, but you know we don't *keep* Christmas; nobody knows anything about Christmas," said the Doctor.

"You know what I mean, my dear," replied his wife. "You know that my mother and her family *do* keep Christmas. I always heard of it when I was a child; and even now, though I have been out of the way of it so long, I cannot help a sort of kindly feeling toward these ways. I am not surprised at all that the children got drawn over last night to the service. I think it's the most natural thing in the world, and I know by experience just how attractive such things are. I shouldn't wonder if this other church should draw very seriously on your congregation; but I don't want it to begin by taking away our own children. Dolly is an inquisitive child; a child that thinks a good deal, and she'll be asking all sorts of questions about the why and wherefore of what she saw last night."

"Oh, yes, Dolly is a bright one. Dolly's an uncommon child," said the Doctor, who had a pardonable pride in his children—they being, in fact, the only worldly treasure that he was at all rich in.

He rose up early on the following Sabbath and proceeded to buy a sugar dog at the store of Lucius Jenks, and when Dolly came down to breakfast he called her to him and presented it, saying as he kissed her:

"Papa gives you this, not because it is Christmas, but because he loves his little Dolly."

"But *isn't* it Christmas?" asked Dolly with a puzzled air.

"No, child; nobody knows when Christ was born, and there is nothing in the Bible to tell us *when* to keep Christmas."

And then in family worship the Doctor read the account of the birth of Christ and of the shepherds abiding in the fields who came at the call of the angels, and they sung the old hymn:

"While shepherds watched their flocks by night."

"Now, children," he said when all was over, "you must be good children and go to school. If we are going to keep any day on account of the birth of Christ, the best way to keep it is by doing all our duties on that day better than any other. Your duty is to be good children, go to school and mind your lessons."

Tom and Bill were quite ready to fall in with their father's view of the matter. As for Dolly, she put her little tongue advisedly to the back of her sugar dog and found that he was very sweet indeed—a most tempting little animal. She even went so far as to nibble off a bit of the green ground he stood on—yet resolved heroically not to eat him at once, but to make him last as long as possible. She wrapped him tenderly in cotton and took him to the school with her, and when her confidential friend, Bessie Lewis, displayed her Christmas gifts, Dolly had something on her side to show, though she shook her curly head and informed Bessie in strict confidence that there wasn't any such thing as Christmas, her papa had told her so—a

189

heresy which Bessie forthwith reported when she went home at noon.

"Poor little child—and did she say so?" asked gentle old Grandmamma Lewis. "Well, dear, you mustn't blame her—she don't know any better. You bring the little one in here to-night and I'll give her a Christmas cooky. I'm sorry for such children."

And so, after school, Dolly went in to see dear old Madam Lewis, who sat in her rocking-chair in the front parlor, where the fire was snapping behind great tall brass andirons and all the pictures were overshadowed with boughs of spruce and pine. Dolly gazed about her with awe and wonder. Over one of the pictures was suspended a cross of green with flowers of white everlasting.

"What is *that* for?" asked Dolly, pointing solemnly with her little forefinger, and speaking under her breath.

"Dear child, that is the picture of my poor boy who died—ever so many years ago. That is my cross—we have all one—to carry."

Dolly did not half understand these words, but she saw tears in the gentle old lady's eyes and was afraid to ask more.

She accepted thankfully and with her nicest and best

executed courtesy a Christmas cooky representing a good-sized fish, with fins all spread and pink sugar-plums for eyes, and went home marveling yet more about this mystery of Christmas.

As she was crossing the green to go home the Poganuc stage drove in, with Hiel seated on high, whipping up his horses to make them execute that grand *entrée* which was the glory of his daily existence.

Now that the stage was on runners, and slipped noiselessly over the smooth frozen plain, Hiel cracked his whip more energetically and shouted louder, first to one horse then to another, to make up for the loss of the rattling wheels; and he generally had the satisfaction of seeing all the women rushing distractedly to doors and windows, and imagined them saying, "There's Hiel; the stage is in!"

"Hulloa, Dolly!" he called out, drawing up with a suddenness which threw the fore-horses back upon their haunches. "I've got a bundle for your folks. Want to ride? You may jest jump up here by me and I'll take you 'round to your father's door"; and so Dolly reached up her little red-mittened hand, and Hiel drew her up beside him.

"'Xpect ye want a bit of a ride, and I've got a bundle

for Widder Badger, down on South Street, so I guess I'll go 'round that way to make it longer. I 'xpect this 'ere bundle is from some of your ma's folks in Boston—'Piscopals they be and keeps Christmas. Good-sized bundle 'tis; reckon it'll come handy in a good many ways."

So, after finishing his detour, Hiel landed his little charge at the parsonage door.

"Reckon I'll be over when I've put up my hosses," he said to Nabby when he handed down the bundle to her. "I hain't been to see you much lately, Nabby, and I know you've been a-pinin' after me, but fact is—"

"Well, now, Hiel Jones, you jest shet up with your imperence," said Nabby, with flashing eyes; "you jest look out or you'll get suthin."

"I 'xpect to get a kiss when I come 'round to-night," said Hiel, composedly. "Take care o' that air bundle, now; mebbe there's glass or crockery in't."

"Hiel Jones," said Nabby, "don't give me none o' your saace, for I won't take it. Jim Sawin said last night you was the brassiest man he ever see. He said there was brass enough in your face to make a kettle of."

"You tell him there's sap enough in his head to fill it,

anyway," said Hiel. "Good bye, Nabby, I'll come 'round this evenin'," and he drove away at a rattling pace, while Nabby, with flushed cheeks and snapping eyes, soliloquized:

"Well, I hope he will come! I'd jest like a chance to show him how little I care for him."

Meanwhile the bundle was soon opened, and contained a store of treasures: a smart little red dress and a pair of red shoes for Dolly, a half dozen pocket-handkerchiefs for Dr. Cushing, and *Robinson Crusoe* and *Sanford and Merton*, handsomely bound, for the boys, and a bonnet trimming for Mrs. Cushing. These were accompanied by a characteristic letter from Aunt Debby Kittery, opening as follows:

"DEAR SISTER:

"Mother worries because she thinks you won't get any Christmas presents. However, this comes to give every one of you some of the crumbs which fall from the church's table, and Mother says she wishes you all a pious Christmas, which she thinks is better than a merry one. If I didn't lay violent hands on her she would use all our substance in riotous giving of Christmas presents to all the beggars and chimney sweeps in

Boston. She is in good health and talks daily of wanting to see you and the children; and I hope before long you will bring some of them, and come and make us a visit.

"Your affectionate sister,

"DEBBY KITTERY."

There was a scene of exultation and clamor in the parsonage as these presents were pulled out and discussed; and when all possible joy was procured from them in the sitting-room, the children rushed in a body into the kitchen and showed them to Nabby, calling on her to join their acclamations.

On the whole, when Dolly had said her prayers that night and thought the matter over, she concluded that her Christmas Day had been quite a success.

The Second Christmas

Once more had Christmas come round in Poganuc; once more the Episcopal church was being dressed with ground-pine and spruce; but this year economy had begun to make its claims felt. An illumination might do very well to open a church, but there were many who said "to what purpose is this waste?" when the proposition was made to renew it yearly. Consequently it was resolved to hold the Christmas Eve service with only that necessary amount of light which would enable the worshipers to read the prayers.

On this Christmas Eve Dolly went to bed at her usual hour with a resigned and quiet spirit. She felt herself a year older, and more than a year wiser, than when Christmas had first dawned upon her consciousness.

Mis' Persis appeared on the ground by day-dawn. A great kettle was slung over the kitchen fire, in which cakes of tallow were speedily liquefying; a frame was placed quite across the kitchen to sustain candle-rods, with a train of boards underneath to catch the drippings, and Mis' Persis, with a brow like one of the Fates, announced: "Now we can't hev any young 'uns in this kitchen to-day"; and Dolly saw that there was no getting any attention in that quarter.

Mis' Persis, in a gracious Saturday afternoon mood, sitting in her own tent-door dispensing hospitalities and cookies, was one thing; but Mis' Persis in her armor, with her loins girded and a hard day's work to be conquered, was quite another: she was terrible as Minerva with her helmet on.

Dinner-baskets for all the children were hastily packed, and they were sent off to school with the injunction on no account to show their faces about the premises till night. The Doctor, warned of what was going on, retreated to his study at the top of the house, where, serenely above the lower cares of earth, he sailed off into President Edwards' treatise on the nature of true virtue, concerning which he was preparing a paper to read at the next association meeting.

That candles were a necessity of life he was well convinced, and by faith he dimly accepted the fact that one day in the year the whole house was to be devoted and given up to this manufacture; and his part of the business, as he understood it, was, clearly, to keep himself out of the way till it was over.

"There won't be much of a dinner at home, anyway," said Nabby to Dolly, as she packed her basket with an extra doughnut or two. "I've got to go to church to-day, 'cause I'm one of the singers, and your ma'll be busy waitin' on *her*; so we shall just have a pick-up dinner, and you be sure not to come home till night; by that time it'll be all over."

Dolly trotted off to school well content with the prospect before her: a nooning, with leave to play with the girls at school, was not an unpleasant idea.

But the first thing that saluted her on her arrival was that Bessie Lewis—her own dear, particular Bessie—was going to have a Christmas party at her house that afternoon, and was around distributing invitations right and left among the scholars with a generous freedom.

"We are going to have nuts, and raisins, and cakes, and mottoes," said Bessie, with artless triumph. The news of this bill of fare spread like wildfire through the school.

Never had a party been heard of which contemplated such a liberal entertainment, for the rising generation of Poganuc were by no means wearied with indulgence, and raisins and almonds stood for grandeur with them. But these *mottoes*, which consisted of bits of confectionery

197

wrapped up in printed couplets of sentimental poetry, were an unheard-of refinement. Bessie assured them that her papa had sent clear to Boston for them, and whoever got one would have his or her fortune told by it.

The school was a small, select one, comprising the children of all ages from the best families of Poganuc. Both boys and girls, and all with great impartiality, had been invited. Miss Titcome, the teacher, quite readily promised to dismiss at three o'clock that afternoon any scholar who should bring a permission from parents, and the children nothing doubted that such a permission was obtainable.

Dolly alone saw a cloud in the horizon. She had been sent away with strict injunctions not to return till evening, and children in those days never presumed to make any exceptions in obeying an absolute command of their parents.

"But, of course, you will go home at noon and ask your mother, and of course she'll let you; won't she, girls?" said Bessie.

"Oh, certainly; of course she will," said all the older girls, "because you know a party is a thing that don't happen every day, and your mother would think it strange if you *didn't* come and ask her." So, too, thought Miss Titcome, a most exemplary, precise and proper young lady, who always moved and spoke and thought as became a schoolmistress, so that, although she was in reality only twenty years old, Dolly considered her as a very advanced and ancient person— if anything, a little older than her father and mother.

Even she was of opinion that Dolly might properly go home to lay a case of such importance before her mother; and so Dolly rushed home after the morning school was over, running with all her might, and increasing in mental excitement as she ran. Her bonnet blew off upon her shoulders, her curls flew behind her in the wind, and she most inconsiderately used up the little stock of breath that she would want to set her cause in order before her mother.

Just here we must beg any mother and housekeeper to imagine herself in the very midst of the most delicate, perplexing and laborious of household tasks, when interruption is most irksome and perilous, suddenly called to discuss with a child some new and startling proposition to which at the moment she cannot even give a thought.

Mrs. Cushing was sitting in the kitchen with Mis' Persis, by the side of a caldron of melted tallow, kept in a fluid state by the heat of a portable furnace on which it stood. A long train of half-dipped candles hung like so many stalactites from the frames on which the rods rested, and the two were patiently dipping set after set and replacing them again on the frame.

"As sure as I'm alive! if there isn't Dolly Cushing comin' back—runnin' and tearin' like a wild cretur'," said Mis' Persis. "She'll be in here in a minute and knock every-thing down!"

Mrs. Cushing looked, and with a quick movement stepped to the door.

"Dolly! what are you here for? Didn't I tell you not to come home this noon?"

"Oh, mamma, there's going to be a party at General Lewis's—Bessie's party—and the girls are all going; mayn't I go?"

"No, you can't; it's impossible," said her mother. "Your best dress isn't ready to wear, and there's nobody can spend time to get you ready. Go right back to school."

"But, mamma—"

"Go!" said her mother, in the decisive tone that mothers used in the old days, when arguing with children was not a possibility.

"What's all this about?" asked the Doctor, looking out of the door.

"Why," said Mrs. Cushing, "there's going to be a party at General Lewis's, and Dolly is wild to go. It's just impossible for me to attend to her now."

"Oh, I don't want her intimate at Lewis's," said the Doctor, and immediately he came out behind his wife.

"There; run away to school, Dolly," he said. "Don't trouble your mother; you don't want to go to parties; why, it's foolish to think of it. Run away now, and don't think any more about it—there's a good girl!"

Dolly turned and went back to school, the tears freezing on her cheek as she went. As for not thinking any more about it—that was impossible.

When three o'clock came, scholar after scholar rose and departed, until at last Dolly was the only one remaining in the school-room.

When Dolly came home that night the coast was clear, and the candles were finished and put away to harden in a freezing cold room; the kitchen was once more restored, and Nabby bustled about getting supper as if nothing had happened.

"I really feel sorry about poor little Dolly," said Mrs. Cushing to her husband.

"Do you think she cared much?" asked the Doctor, looking as if a new possibility had struck his mind.

"Yes, indeed, poor child, she went away crying; but what could I do about it? I couldn't stop to dress her."

"Wife, we must take her somewhere to make up for it," said the Doctor.

Just then the stage stopped at the door and a bundle from Boston was handed in. Dolly's tears were soon wiped and dried, and her mourning was turned into joy when a large jointed London doll emerged from the bundle, the Christmas gift of her grandmother in Boston.

Dolly's former darling was old and shabby, but this was of twice the size, and with cheeks exhibiting a state of the most florid health.

Besides this there was, as usual in grandmamma's Christmas bundle, something for every member of the family; and so the evening went on festive wings.

Poor little Dolly! only that afternoon she had watered with her tears, at school, the dismal long straight seam, which stretched on before her as life sometimes does to us, bare, disagreeable and cheerless. She had come home crying, little dreaming of the joy just approaching; but before bed-time no cricket in the hearth was cheerier or more noisy. She took the new dolly to bed with her, and could hardly sleep, for the excitement of her company.

Meanwhile, Hiel had brought the Doctor a message to the following effect:

"I was drivin' by Tim Hawkins', and Mis' Hawkins she comes out and says they're goin' to hev an apple-cuttin' there to-morrow night, and she would like to hev you and Mis' Cushin' and all your folks come—Nabby and all."

The Doctor and his lady of course assented.

"Wal, then, Doctor—ef it's all one to you," continued Hiel, "I'd like to take ye over in my new double sleigh. I've jest got two new strings o' bells up from Boston, and I think we'll sort o' make the snow fly. S'pose there'd be no objections to takin' my mother 'long with ye?"

"Oh, Hiel, we shall be delighted to go in company with your mother, and we're ever so much obliged to you," said Mrs. Cushing.

"Wal, I'll be round by six o'clock," said Hiel.

"Then, wife," said the Doctor, "we'll take Dolly, and make up for the loss of her party."

Punctually at six, Hiel's two horses, with all their bells jingling, stood at the door of the parsonage, whence Tom and Bill, who had been waiting with caps and mittens on for the last half hour, burst forth with irrepressible shouts of welcome.

"Take care now, boys; don't haul them buffalo skins out on t' the snow," said Hiel. "Don't get things in a muss gen'ally; wait for your ma and the Doctor. Got to stow the grown folks in fust; boys kin hang on anywhere."

And so first came Mrs. Cushing and the Doctor, and were installed on the back seat, with Dolly in between. Then hot bricks were handed in to keep feet warm, and the buffalo robe was tucked down securely. Then Nabby took her seat by Hiel in front, and the sleigh drove round for old Mrs. Jones. The Doctor insisted on giving up his place to her and tucking her warmly under the buffalo robe, while he took the middle seat and acted as moderator between the boys, who were in a wild state of hilarity. Spring, with explosive barks, raced first on this and then on that side of the sleigh as it flew swiftly over the smooth frozen road.

The stars blinked white and clear out of a deep blue sky, and the path wound up-hill among cedars and junipers and clumps of mountain laurel, on whose broad green leaves the tufts of snow lay like clusters of white roses. The keen clear air was full of stimulus and vigor; and so Hiel's proposition to take the longest way met with enthusiastic welcome from all the party. Next to being a bird, and having wings, is the sensation of being borne over the snow by a pair of spirited horses who enjoy the race, apparently, as much as those they draw. Though Hiel contrived to make the ride about eight miles, it yet seemed but a short time before the party drove up to the great red farmhouse, whose lighted windows sent streams of radiant welcome far out into the night.

Our little Dolly had had an evening of unmixed bliss. Everybody had petted her, and talked to her, and been delighted with her sayings and doings, and she was carrying home a paper parcel of sweet things which good Mrs. Hawkins had forced into her hand at parting. She had spent a really happy Christmas!

Charles Dickens

1812–1870

A CHRISTMAS DINNER

Christmas time! That man must be a misanthrope indeed, in whose breast something like a jovial feeling is not roused—in whose mind some pleasant associations are not awakened—by the recurrence of Christmas. There are people who will tell you that Christmas is not to them what it used to be; that each succeeding Christmas has found some cherished hope, or happy prospect, of the year before, dimmed or passed away; that the present only serves to remind them of reduced circumstances and straitened incomes—of the feasts they once bestowed on hollow friends, and of the cold looks that meet them now, in adversity and misfortune. Never heed such dismal reminiscences. There are few men who have lived long enough in the world, who cannot call up such thoughts any day in the year. Then do not select the merriest of the three hundred and sixty-five for your doleful recollections, but draw your chair nearer the blazing fire—fill the glass and send round the song—and if your room be smaller than it was a dozen years ago, or if your glass be filled with reeking punch, instead of sparkling wine, put a good face on the matter, and empty it off-hand, and fill another, and troll off the old ditty you used to sing, and thank God it's no worse. Look on the merry faces of your children (if you have any) as they sit round the fire. One little seat may be empty; one slight form that gladdened the father's heart, and roused the mother's pride to look upon, may not be there. Dwell not upon the past; think not that one short year ago, the fair child now resolving into dust, sat before you, with the bloom of health upon its cheek, and the gaiety of infancy in its joyous eye. Reflect upon your present blessings—of which every man has many—not on your past misfortunes, of which all men have some. Fill your glass again, with a merry face and contented heart. Our life on it, but your Christmas shall be merry, and your new year a happy one!

Who can be insensible to the outpourings of good feeling, and the honest interchange of affectionate attachment, which abound at this season of the year? A Christmas family-party! We know nothing in nature more delightful! There seems a magic in the very name of Christmas. Petty jealousies and discords are forgotten; social feelings are awakened, in bosoms to which they have long been strangers; father and son, or brother and sister, who have met and passed with averted gaze, or a look of cold recognition, for months before, proffer and return the cordial embrace, and bury their past animosities in their present happiness. Kindly hearts that have yearned towards each other, but have been withheld by false notions of pride and self-dignity, are again reunited, and all is kindness and benevolence! Would that Christmas lasted the whole year through (as it ought), and that the prejudices and passions which deform our better nature, were never called into action among those to whom they should ever be strangers!

The Christmas family-party that we mean, is not a mere assemblage of relations, got up at a week or two's notice, originating this year, having no family precedent in the last, and not likely to be repeated in the next. No. It is an annual gathering of all the accessible members of the family, young or old, rich or poor; and all the children look forward to it, for two months beforehand, in a fever of anticipation. Formerly, it was held at grandpapa's; but grandpapa getting old, and grandmamma getting old too, and rather infirm, they have given up house-keeping, and domesticated themselves with uncle George; so, the party always takes place at uncle George's house, but grandmamma sends in most of the good things, and grandpapa always *will* toddle down, all the way to Newgate-market, to buy the turkey, which he engages a porter to bring home behind him in triumph, always insisting on the man's being rewarded with a glass of spirits, over and above his hire, to drink "a merry Christmas and a happy new year" to aunt George. As to grandmamma, she is very secret and mysterious for two or three days beforehand, but not sufficiently so, to prevent rumours getting afloat that she has purchased a beautiful new cap with pink ribbons for each of the servants, together with sundry books, and pen-knives, and pencil-cases, for the younger branches; to say nothing of divers secret additions to the order originally given by aunt George at the pastry-cook's, such as another dozen of mince-pies for the dinner, and a large plum-cake for the children.

On Christmas-eve, grandmamma is always in excellent

spirits, and after employing all the children, during the day, in stoning the plums, and all that, insists, regularly every year, on uncle George coming down into the kitchen, taking off his coat, and stirring the pudding for half an hour or so, which uncle George good-humouredly does, to the vociferous delight of the children and servants. The evening concludes with a glorious game of blind-man's-buff, in an early stage of which grandpapa takes great care to be caught, in order that he may have an opportunity of displaying his dexterity.

On the following morning, the old couple, with as many of the children as the pew will hold, go to church in great state: leaving aunt George at home dusting decanters and filling casters, and uncle George carrying bottles into the dining-parlour, and calling for corkscrews, and getting into everybody's way.

When the church-party return to lunch, grandpapa produces a small sprig of mistletoe from his pocket, and tempts the boys to kiss their little cousins under it—a proceeding which affords both the boys and the old gentleman unlimited satisfaction, but which rather outrages grandmamma's ideas of decorum, until grandpapa says, that when he was

just thirteen years and three months old, *he* kissed grandmamma under a mistletoe too, on which the children clap
their hands, and laugh very heartily, as do aunt George and
uncle George; and grandmamma looks pleased, and says,
with a benevolent smile, that grandpapa was an impudent
young dog, on which the children laugh very heartily again,
and grandpapa more heartily than any of them.

But all these diversions are nothing to the subsequent
excitement when grandmamma in a high cap, and slate-
coloured silk gown; and grandpapa with a beautifully
plaited shirt-frill, and white neckerchief; seat themselves
on one side of the drawing-room fire, with uncle George's
children and little cousins innumerable, seated in the
front, waiting the arrival of the expected visitors. Suddenly
a hackney-coach is heard to stop, and uncle George, who
has been looking out of the window, exclaims "Here's
Jane!" on which the children rush to the door, and helter-
skelter down stairs; and uncle Robert and aunt Jane, and
the dear little baby, and the nurse, and the whole party, are
ushered up stairs amidst tumultuous shouts of "Oh, my!"
from the children, and frequently repeated warnings not to
hurt baby from the nurse. And grandpapa takes the child,

and grandmamma kisses her daughter, and the confusion of this first entry has scarcely subsided, when some other aunts and uncles with more cousins arrive, and the grown-up cousins flirt with each other, and so do the little cousins too, for that matter, and nothing is to be heard but a confused din of talking, laughing, and merriment.

A hesitating double knock at the street-door, heard during a momentary pause in the conversation, excites a general inquiry of "Who's that?" and two or three children, who have been standing at the window, announce in a low voice, that it's "poor aunt Margaret." Upon which, aunt George leaves the room to welcome the new-comer; and grandmamma draws herself up, rather stiff and stately; for Margaret married a poor man without her consent, and poverty not being a sufficiently weighty punishment for her offence, has been discarded by her friends, and debarred the society of her dearest relatives. But Christmas has come round, and the unkind feelings that have struggled against better dispositions during the year, have melted away before its genial influence, like half-formed ice beneath the morning sun. It is not difficult in a moment of angry feeling for a parent to denounce a disobedient child; but, to banish her at a period of general good-will and hilarity, from the hearth, round which she has sat on so many anniversaries of the same day, expanding by slow degrees from infancy to girlhood, and then bursting, almost imperceptibly, into a woman, is widely different. The air of conscious rectitude, and cold forgiveness, which the old lady has assumed, sits ill upon her; and when the poor girl is led in by her sister, pale in looks and broken in hope—not from poverty, for that she could bear, but from the consciousness of undeserved neglect, and unmerited unkindness—it is easy to see how much of it is assumed. A momentary pause succeeds; the girl breaks suddenly from her sister and throws herself, sobbing, on her mother's neck. The father steps hastily forward, and takes her husband's hand. Friends crowd round to offer their hearty congratulations, and happiness and harmony again prevail.

As to the dinner, it's perfectly delightful—nothing goes wrong, and everybody is in the very best of spirits, and disposed to please and be pleased. Grandpapa relates a circumstantial account of the purchase of the turkey, with a slight digression relative to the purchase of previous turkeys, on former Christmas-days, which grandmamma corroborates in the minutest particular. Uncle George tells stories, and carves poultry, and takes wine, and jokes with the children at the side-table, and winks at the cousins that are making love, or being made love to, and exhilarates everybody with his good humour and hospitality; and when, at last, a stout servant staggers in with a gigantic pudding, with a sprig of holly in the top, there is such a laughing, and shouting, and clapping of little chubby hands, and kicking up of fat dumpy legs, as can only be equalled by the applause with which the astonishing feat of pouring lighted brandy into mince-pies, is received by the younger visitors. Then the dessert!—and the wine!—and the fun! Such beautiful speeches, and *such* songs, from aunt Margaret's husband, who turns out to be such a nice man, and *so* attentive to grandmamma! Even grandpapa not only sings his annual song with unprecedented vigour, but on being honoured with an unanimous *encore*, according to annual custom, actually comes out with a new one which nobody but grandmamma ever heard before; and a young scapegrace of a cousin, who has been in some disgrace with the old people, for certain heinous sins of omission and commission—neglecting to call, and persisting in drinking Burton Ale—astonishes everybody into convulsions of laughter by volunteering the most extraordinary comic songs that ever were heard. And thus the evening passes, in a strain of rational good-will and cheerfulness, doing more to awaken the sympathies of every member of the party in behalf of his neighbour, and to perpetuate their good feeling during the ensuing year, than half the homilies that have ever been written, by half the Divines that have ever lived.

Mark Twain

. . . .

1835–1910

A LETTER FROM SANTA CLAUS

PALACE OF ST. NICHOLAS
IN THE MOON
CHRISTMAS MORNING

My Dear Susie Clemens,

I have received and read all the letters which you
and your little sister have written me . . . I can read
your and your baby sister's jagged and fantastic marks
without any trouble at all. But I had trouble with
those letters which you dictated through your mother
and the nurses, for I am a foreigner and cannot read
English writing well. You will find that I made no mistakes about the things which you and the baby ordered
in your own letters—I went down your chimney at

midnight when you were asleep and delivered them all myself—and kissed both of you, too . . . But . . . there were . . . one or two small orders which I could not fill because we ran out of stock . . .

There was a word or two in your mama's letter which . . . I took to be "a trunk full of doll's clothes." Is that it? I will call at your kitchen door about nine o'clock this morning to inquire. But I must not see any-body and I must not speak to anybody but you. When the kitchen doorbell rings, George must be blindfolded and sent to the door.

You must tell George he must walk on tiptoe and not speak—otherwise he will die someday. Then you must go up to the nursery and stand on a chair or the nurse's bed and put your ear to the speaking tube that leads down to the kitchen and when I whistle through it you must speak in the tube and say, "Welcome, Santa Claus!" Then I will ask whether it was a trunk you ordered or not. If you say it was, I shall ask you what color you want the trunk to be . . . and then you must tell me every single thing in detail which you want the trunk to contain. Then when I say "Good-by and a merry Christmas to my little Susie Clemens," you must say "Good-by, good old Santa Claus, I thank you very much." Then you must go down into the library and make George close all the doors that open into the main hall, and everybody must keep still for a little while. I will go to the moon and get those things and in a few minutes I will come down the chimney that belongs to the fireplace that is in the hall—if it is a trunk you want—because I couldn't get such a thing as a trunk down the nursery chimney, you know . . . If I should leave any snow in the hall, you must tell George to sweep it into the fireplace, for I haven't time to do such things.

George must not use a broom, but a rag—else he will die someday . . . If my boot should leave a stain on the marble, George must not holystone it away. Leave it there always in memory of my visit; and whenever you look at it or show it to anybody you must let it remind you to be a good little girl. Whenever you are naughty and someone points to that mark which your good old Santa Claus's boot made on the marble, what will you say, little sweetheart?

Good-by for a few minutes, till I come down to the world and ring the kitchen doorbell.

Your loving Santa Claus
Whom people
sometimes call "The
Man in the Moon"

Kate Douglas Wiggin
and Nora A. Smith

1856–1923 / 1859–1934

THE STORY OF CHRISTMAS

Christmas Day, you knew, dear children, is Christ's day, Christ's birthday, and I want to tell you why we love it so much, and why we try to make every one happy when it comes each year.

A long, long time ago—more than eighteen hundred years—the baby Christ was born on Christmas Day: a baby so wonderful and so beautiful, who grew up to be a man so wise, so good, so patient and sweet, that, every year, the people who know about him love him better and better, and are more and more glad when his birthday comes again. You see that he must have been very good and wonderful; for people have always remembered his birthday, and kept it lovingly for eighteen hundred years.

He was born, long years ago, in a land far, far away across the seas.

Before the baby Christ was born, Mary, his mother, had to make a long journey with her husband, Joseph. They made this journey to be taxed or counted; for in those days this could not be done in the town where people happened to live, but they must be numbered in the place where they were born.

In that far-off time, the only way of traveling was on a horse, or a camel, or a good, patient donkey. Camels and horses cost a great deal of money, and Mary was very poor; so she rode on a quiet, safe donkey, while Joseph walked by her side, leading him and leaning on his stick. Mary was very young, and beautiful, I think, but Joseph was a great deal older than she.

People dress nowadays, in those distant countries, just as they did so many years ago, so we know that Mary must have worn a long, thick dress, falling all about her in heavy folds, and that she had a soft white veil over her head and neck, and across her face. Mary lived in Nazareth, and the journey they were making was to Bethlehem, many miles away.

They were a long time traveling, I am sure; for donkeys are slow, though they are so careful, and Mary must have been very tired before they came to the end of their journey.

They had traveled all day, and it was almost dark when they came near to Bethlehem, to the town where the baby Christ was to be born. There was the place they were to stay,—a kind of inn, or lodging-house, but not at all like those you know about.

They have them to-day in that far-off country, just as they built them so many years ago.

It was a low, flat-roofed, stone building, with no window and only one large door. There were no nicely furnished bedrooms inside, and no soft white beds for the tired travelers; there were only little places built into the stones of the wall, something like the berths on steamboats nowadays, and each traveler brought his own bedding. No pretty garden was in front of the inn, for the road ran close to the very door, so that its dust lay upon the doorsill. All around the house, to a high, rocky hill at the back, a heavy stone fence was built, so that the people and the animals inside might be kept safe.

Mary and Joseph could not get very near the inn; for the

whole road in front was filled with camels and donkeys and sheep and cows, while a great many men were going to and fro, taking care of the animals. Some of these people had come to Bethlehem to pay their taxes, as Mary and Joseph had done, and others were staying for the night, on their way to Jerusalem, a large city a little further on.

The yard was filled, too, with camels and sheep; and men were lying on the ground beside them, resting, and watching, and keeping them safe. The inn was so full and the yard was so full of people, that there was no room for anybody else, and the keeper had to take Joseph and Mary through the house and back to the high hill, where they found another place that was used for a stable. This had only a door and a front, and deep caves were behind, stretching far into the rocks.

This was the spot where Christ was born. Think how poor a place!—but Mary was glad to be there, after all; and when the Christ-child came, he was like other babies, and had so lately come from heaven that he was happy everywhere.

There were mangers all around the cave, where the cattle and sheep were fed, and great heaps of hay and straw were lying on the floor. Then, I think, there were brown-eyed cows and oxen there, and quiet, woolly sheep, and perhaps even some dogs that had come in to take care of the sheep.

And there in the cave, by and by, the wonderful baby came, and they wrapped him up and laid him in a manger.

All the stars in the sky shone brightly that night, for they knew the Christ-child was born, and the angels in heaven sang together for joy. The angels knew about the lovely child, and were glad that he had come to help the people on earth to be good.

There lay the beautiful baby, with a manger for his bed, and oxen and sheep all sleeping quietly round him. His mother watched him and loved him, and by and by many people came to see him, for they had heard that a wonderful child was to be born in Bethlehem. All the people in the inn visited him, and even the shepherds left their flocks in the fields and sought the child and his mother.

But the baby was very tiny, and could not talk any more than any other tiny child, so he lay in his mother's lap, or in the manger, and only looked at the people. So after they had seen him and loved him, they went away again.

After a time, when the baby had grown larger, Mary took him back to Nazareth, and there he lived and grew up.

And he grew to be such a sweet, wise, loving boy, such a tender, helpful man, and he said so many good and beautiful things, that every one loved him who knew him. Many of the things he said are in the Bible, you know, and a great many beautiful stories of the things he used to do while he was on earth.

He loved little children like you very much, and often used to take them up in his arms and talk to them.

And this is the reason we love Christmas Day so much, and try to make everybody happy when it comes around each year. This is the reason: because Christ, who was born on Christmas Day, has helped us all to be good so many, many times, and because he was the best Christmas present the great world ever had!

Ralph Henry Barbour

1870–1944

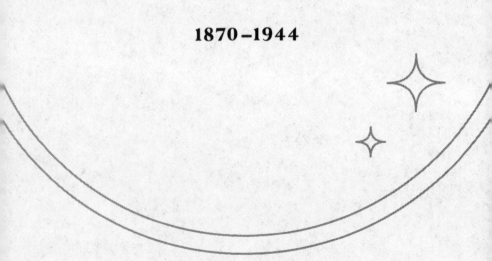

A COLLEGE SANTA CLAUSE

Satherwaite, '02, threw his overcoat across the broad mahogany table, regardless of the silver and cutglass furnishings, shook the melting snowflakes from his cap and tossed it atop the coat, half kicked, half shoved a big leathern arm-chair up to the wide fireplace, dropped himself into it, and stared moodily at the flames.

Satherwaite was troubled. In fact, he assured himself, drawing his handsome features into a generous scowl, that he was, on this Christmas eve, the most depressed and bored person in the length and breadth of New England. Satherwaite was not used to being depressed, and boredom was a state usually far remote from his experience; consequently, he took it worse. With something between a groan and a growl, he drew a crumpled telegram from his pocket. The telegram was at the bottom of it all. He read it again:

R. SATHERWAITE,

Randolph Hall, Cambridge.

Advise your not coming. Aunt Louise very ill.

Merry Christmas.

PHIL.

"'Merry Christmas!'" growled Satherwaite, throwing the offending sheet of buff paper into the flames. "Looks like it, doesn't it? Confound Phil's Aunt Louise, anyway! What business has she getting sick at Christmas time? Not, of course, that I wish the old lady any harm, but it—it—well, it's wretched luck."

When at college, Phil was the occupant of the bedroom that lay in darkness beyond the half-opened door to the right. He lived, when at home, in a big, rambling house in the Berkshires, a house from the windows of which one could see into three states and overlook a wonderful expanse of wooded hill and sloping meadow; a house which held, beside Phil, and Phil's father and mother and Aunt

Louise and a younger brother, Phil's sister. Satherwaite growled again, more savagely, at the thought of Phil's sister; not, be it understood, at that extremely attractive young lady, but at the fate which was keeping her from his sight.

Satherwaite had promised his roommate to spend Christmas with him, thereby bringing upon himself pained remonstrances from his own family, remonstrances which, Satherwaite acknowledged, were quite justifiable. His bags stood beside the door. He had spent the early afternoon very pleasurably in packing them, carefully weighing the respective merits of a primrose waistcoat and a blue flannel one, as weapons wherewith to impress the heart of Phil's sister. And now—!

He kicked forth his feet, and brought brass tongs and shovel clattering on the hearth. It relieved his exasperation.

The fatal telegram had reached him at five o'clock, as he was on the point of donning his coat. From five to six, he had remained in a torpor of disappointment, smoking pipe after pipe, and continually wondering whether Phil's sister would care. At six, his own boarding-house being closed for the recess, he had trudged through the snow to a restaurant in the square, and had dined miserably on lukewarm turkey and lumpy mashed potatoes. And now it was nearly eight, and he did not even care to smoke. His one chance of reaching his own home that night had passed, and there was nothing for it but to get through the interminable evening somehow, and catch an early train in the morning. The theatres in town offered no attraction. As for his club, he had stopped in on his way from dinner, and had fussed with an evening paper, until the untenanted expanse of darkly-furnished apartments and the unaccustomed stillness had driven him forth again.

He drew his long legs under him, and arose, crossing the room and drawing aside the deep-toned hangings before the window. It was still snowing. Across the avenue, a flood of mellow light from a butcher's shop was thrown out over the snowy sidewalk. Its windows were garlanded with Christmas greens and hung with pathetic-looking turkeys and geese. Belated shoppers passed out, their arms piled high with bundles. A car swept by, its drone muffled by the snow. The spirit of Christmas was in the very air. Satherwaite's depression increased and, of a sudden, inaction became intolerable. He would go and see somebody, anybody, and make them talk to him; but, when he had his coat in his hands, he realized that even this comfort was denied him. He had friends in town, nice folk who would be glad to see him any other time, but into whose family gatherings he could no more force himself to-night than he could steal. As for the men he knew in college, they had all gone to their homes or to those of somebody else.

Staring disconsolately about the study, it suddenly struck him that the room looked disgustingly slovenly and unkempt. Phil was such an untidy beggar! He would fix things up a bit. If he did it carefully and methodically, no doubt he could consume a good hour and a half that way. It would then be half-past nine. Possibly, if he tried hard, he could use up another hour bathing and getting ready for bed. And at half-past ten lots of fellows went to sleep. He could not remember having done so himself of late years, but he could try it; and, if he succeeded, it would be a good joke to tell Phil—confound him!

As a first step, he removed his coat from the table, and laid it carefully across the foot of the leather couch. Then he placed his damp cap on one end of the mantel. The next object to meet his gaze was a well-worn note-book. It was not his own, and it did not look like Phil's. The mystery was solved when he opened it and read, "H. G. Doyle—College House," on the fly-leaf. He remembered then. He had borrowed it from Doyle almost a week before, at a lecture. He had copied some of the notes, and had forgotten to return the book. It was very careless of him; he would return it as soon as—Then he recollected having seen Doyle at noon that day, coming from one of the cheaper boarding-houses. It was probable that Doyle was spending recess at college. Just the thing—he would call on Doyle!

It was not until he was half-way down-stairs that he remembered the book. He went back for it, two steps at a time. Out in the street, with the fluffy flakes against his face, he felt better. After all, there was no use in getting grouchy over his disappointment; Phil would keep; and so would Phil's sister, at least until Easter; or, better yet, he would get Phil to take him home with him over Sunday some time. He was passing the shops now, and stopped before a jeweler's window, his eye caught by a rather jolly-looking paper-knife in gun-metal. He had made his purchases for Christmas and had already dispatched them, but the paper-knife looked attractive and, if there was no one to give it to, he could keep it himself. So he passed into the shop, and purchased it.

"Put it into a box, will you?" he requested. "I may want to send it away."

Out on the avenue again, his thoughts reverted to his prospective host. The visit had elements of humor. He had known Doyle at preparatory school, and since then, at college, had maintained the acquaintance in a casual way. He liked Doyle, always had, just as any man must like an honest, earnest, gentlemanly fellow, whether their paths run parallel or cross only at rare intervals. He and Doyle were not at all in the same coterie. Satherwaite's friends were the richest, and sometimes the laziest, men in college; Doyle's were—well, presumably men who, like himself, had only enough money to scrape through from September to June, who studied hard for degrees, whose viewpoint of university life must, of necessity, be widely separated from Satherwaite's. As for visiting Doyle, Satherwaite could not remember ever having been in his room but once, and that was long ago, in their Freshman year.

Satherwaite had to climb two flights of steep and very narrow stairs, and when he stood at Doyle's door, he thought he must have made a mistake. From within came the sounds of very unstudious revelry, laughter, a snatch of song, voices raised in good-natured argument. Satherwaite referred again to the fly-leaf of the note-book; there was no error. He knocked and, in obedience to a cheery, "Come in!" entered.

He found himself in a small study, shabbily furnished, but cheerful and homelike by reason of the leaping flames in the grate and the blue haze of tobacco-smoke that almost hid its farther wall. About the room sat six men, their pipes held questioningly away from their mouths and their eyes fixed wonderingly, half-resentfully, upon the intruder. But what caught and held Satherwaite's gaze was a tiny Christmas tree, scarcely three feet high, which adorned the centre of the desk. Its branches held toy candles, as yet unlighted, and were festooned with strings of crimson cranberries and colored popcorn, while here and there a small package dangled amid the greenery.

"How are you, Satherwaite?"

Doyle, tall, lank and near-sighted, arose and moved forward, with outstretched hand. He was plainly embarrassed, as was every other occupant of the study, Satherwaite included. The laughter and talk had subsided. Doyle's guests politely removed their gaze from the new-comer, and returned their pipes to their lips. But the new-comer was intruding, and knew it, and he was consequently embarrassed. Embarrassment, like boredom, was a novel sensation to him, and he speedily decided that he did not fancy it. He held out Doyle's book.

"I brought this back, old man. I don't know how I came to forget it. I'm awfully sorry, you know; it was so very decent of you to lend it to me. Awfully sorry, really."

Doyle murmured that it didn't matter, not a particle; and wouldn't Satherwaite sit down?

No, Satherwaite couldn't stop. He heard the youth in the faded cricket-blazer tell the man next to him, in a stage aside, that this was "Satherwaite, '02, an awful swell, you know." Satherwaite again declared that he could not remain.

Doyle said he was sorry; they were just having a little—a sort of a Christmas-eve party, you know. He blushed while he explained, and wondered whether Satherwaite thought them a lot of idiots, or simply a parcel of sentimental kids. Probably, Satherwaite knew some of the fellows? he went on.

Satherwaite studied the assemblage, and replied that he thought not, though he remembered having seen several of them at lectures and things. Doyle made no move toward introducing his friends to Satherwaite, and, to relieve the momentary silence that followed, observed that he supposed it was getting colder. Satherwaite replied, absently, that he hadn't noticed, but that it was still snowing. The youth in the cricket-blazer fidgeted in his chair. Satherwaite was thinking.

Of course, he was not wanted there; he realized that. Yet, he was of half a mind to stay. The thought of his empty room dismayed him. The cheer and comfort before him appealed to him forcibly. And, more than all, he was possessed of a desire to vindicate himself to this circle of narrow-minded critics. Great Scott! just because he had some money and went with some other fellows who also had money, he was to be promptly labeled "cad," and treated with polite tolerance only. By Jove, he would stay, if only to punish them for their narrowness!

"You're sure I sha'n't be intruding, Doyle?" he asked.

Doyle gasped in amazement. Satherwaite removed his coat. A shiver of consternation passed through the room. Then the host found his tongue.

"Glad to have you. Nothing much doing. Few friends. Quiet evening. Let me take your coat."

Introductions followed. The man in the cricket-blazer turned out to be Doak, '03, the man who had won the Jonas Greeve scholarship; a small youth with eagle-like countenance was Somers, he who had debated so brilliantly against Princeton; a much-bewhiskered man was Ailworth, of the Law School; Kranch and Smith, both members of Satherwaite's class, completed the party. Satherwaite shook hands with those within reach, and looked for a chair. Instantly, every one was on his feet; there was a confused chorus of, "Take this, won't you?" Satherwaite accepted a straight-backed chair with part of its cane seat missing, after a decent amount of protest; then a heavy, discouraging silence fell. Satherwaite looked around the circle. Everyone save Ailworth and Doyle was staring blankly at the fire. Ailworth dropped his eyes, gravely; Doyle broke out explosively with:

"Do you smoke, Satherwaite?"

"Yes, but I'm afraid"—he searched his pockets, perfunctorily—"I haven't my pipe with me." His cigarette-case met his searching fingers, but somehow cigarettes did not seem appropriate.

"I'm sorry," said Doyle, "but I'm afraid I haven't an extra one. Any of you fellows got a pipe that's not working?"

Murmured regrets followed. Doak, who sat next to Satherwaite, put a hand in his coat pocket, and viewed the intruder doubtingly, from around the corners of his glasses.

"It doesn't matter a bit," remarked Satherwaite, heartily.

"I've got a sort of a pipe here," said Doak, "if you're not over particular what you smoke."

Satherwaite received the pipe gravely. It was a blackened briar, whose bowl was burned half-way down on one side, from being lighted over the gas, and whose mouthpiece, gnawed away in long usage, had been re-shaped with a knife. Satherwaite examined it with interest, rubbing the bowl gently on his knee. He knew, without seeing, that Doak was eying him with mingled defiance and apology, and wondering in what manner a man who was used to meerschaums and gold-mounted briars would take the proffer of his worn-out favorite; and he knew, too, that all the others were watching. He placed the stem between his lips, and drew on it once or twice, with satisfaction.

"It seems a jolly old pipe," he said; "I fancy you must be rather fond of it. Has anyone got any 'baccy?"

Five pouches were tendered instantly.

Satherwaite filled his pipe, carefully. He had won the

first trick, he told himself, and the thought was pleasurable. The conversation had started up again, but it was yet perfunctory, and Satherwaite realized that he was still an outsider. Doyle gave him the opportunity he wanted.

"Isn't it something new for you to stay here through recess?" he asked.

Then Satherwaite told about Phil's Aunt Louise and the telegram; about his dismal dinner at the restaurant and the subsequent flight from the tomb-like silence of the club; how he had decided, in desperation, to clean up his study, and how he had come across Doyle's note-book. He told it rather well; he had a reputation for that sort of thing, and to-night he did his best. He pictured himself to his audience on the verge of suicide from melancholia, and assured them that this fate had been averted only through his dislike of being found lifeless amid such untidy surroundings. He decked the narrative with touches of drollery, and was rewarded with the grins that overspread the faces of his hearers. Ailworth nodded appreciatively, now and then, and Doak even slapped his knee once and giggled aloud. Satherwaite left out all mention of Phil's sister, naturally, and ended with:

"And so, when I saw you fellows having such a Christian, comfortable sort of a time, I simply couldn't break away again. I knew I was risking getting myself heartily disliked, and, really, I wouldn't blame you if you arose *en masse* and kicked me out. But I am desperate. Give me some tobacco from time to time, and just let me sit here and listen to you; it will be a kindly act to a homeless orphan."

"Shut up!" said Doyle, heartily; "we're glad to have you, of course." The others concurred. "We—we're going to light up the tree after a bit. We do it every year, you know. It's kind of—of Christmassy when you don't get home for the holidays, you see. We give one another little presents and—and have rather a bit of fun out of it. Only"—he hesitated doubtfully—"only, I'm afraid it may bore you awfully."

"Bore me!" cried Satherwaite; "why, man alive, I should think it would be the jolliest sort of a thing. It's just like being boys again." He turned and observed the tiny tree with interest.

"And do you mean that you all give one another presents, and keep it secret, and—and all that?"

"Yes; just little things, you know," answered Doak, deprecatingly.

"It's the nearest thing to a real Christmas that I've known for seven years," said Ailworth, gravely. Satherwaite observed him, wonderingly.

"By Jove!" he murmured; "seven years! Do you know, I'm glad now I am going home, instead of to Sterner's for Christmas. A fellow ought to be with his own folks, don't you think?"

Everybody said, yes, heartily, and there was a moment of silence in the room. Presently Kranch, whose home was in Michigan, began speaking reminiscently of the Christmases he had spent when a lad in the pine woods. He made the others feel the cold and the magnitude of the pictures he drew, and, for a space, Satherwaite was transported to a little lumber town in a clearing, and stood by excitedly, while a small boy in jeans drew woolen mittens—wonderful ones of red and gray—from out a Christmas stocking. And Somers told of a Christmas he had once spent in a Quebec village; and Ailworth followed him with an account of Christmas morning in a Maine-coast fishing town.

Satherwaite was silent. He had no Christmases of his own to tell about; they would have been sorry, indeed, after the others; Christmases in a big Philadelphia house, rather staid and stupid days, as he remembered them now, days lacking in any delightful element of uncertainty, but filled with wonderful presents so numerous that the novelty had worn away from them ere bedtime. He felt that, somehow, he had been cheated out of a pleasure which should have been his.

The tobacco-pouches went from hand to hand. Christmas-giving had already begun; and Satherwaite, to avoid disappointing his new friends, had to smoke many more pipes than was good for him. Suddenly, they found themselves in darkness, save for the firelight. Doyle had arisen stealthily and turned out the gas. Then, one by one, the tiny candles flickered and flared bluely into flame. Some one pulled the shades from before the two windows, and the room was hushed. Outside, they could see the flakes falling, silently, steadily, between them and the electric lights that shone across the avenue. It was a beautiful, cold, still world of blue mists. A gong clanged softly, and a car, well-nigh untenanted, slid by beneath them, its windows, frosted half-way up, flooding the snow with mellow light. Some one beside Satherwaite murmured, gently:

"Good old Christmas!"

The spell was broken. Satherwaite sighed—why, he hardly knew—and turned away from the window. The tree was brilliantly lighted now, and the strings of cranberries caught the beams ruddily. Doak stirred the fire, and Doyle, turning from a whispered consultation with some of the others, approached Satherwaite.

"Would you mind playing Santa Claus—give out the presents, you know; we always do it that way?"

Satherwaite would be delighted; and, better to impersonate that famous old gentleman, he turned up the collar of his jacket, and put each hand up the opposite sleeve, looking as benignant as possible the while.

"That's fine!" cried Smith; "but hold on, you need a cap!"

He seized one from the window-seat, a worn thing of yellowish-brown otter, and drew it down over Satherwaite's ears. The crowd applauded, merrily.

"Dear little boys and girls," began Satherwaite, in a quavering voice.

"No girls!" cried Doak.

"I want the cranberries!" cried Smith; "I love cranberries."

"I get the popcorn, then!" That was the sedate Ailworth.

"You'll be beastly sick," said Doak, grinning jovially through his glasses.

Satherwaite untied the first package from its twig. It bore the inscription, "For Little Willie Kranch." Every one gathered around while the recipient undid the wrappings, and laid bare a pen-wiper adorned with a tiny crimson football. Doak explained to Satherwaite that Kranch had played football just once, on a scrub team, and had heroically carried the ball down a long field, and placed it triumphantly under his own goal posts. This accounted for the laughter that ensued.

"Sammy Doak" received a note-book marked "Mathematics 3a." The point of this allusion was lost to Satherwaite, for Doak was too busy laughing to explain it. And so it went, and the room was in a constant roar of mirth. Doyle was conferring excitedly with Ailworth across the room. By and by, he stole forward, and, detaching one of the packages from the tree, erased and wrote on it with great secrecy. Then he tied it back again, and retired to the hearth, grinning expectantly, until his own name was called, and he was shoved forward to receive a rubber pen-holder.

Presently, Satherwaite, working around the Christmas tree, detached a package, and frowned over the address.

"Fellows, this looks like—like Satherwaite, but"—he viewed the assemblage in embarrassment—"but I fancy it's a mistake."

"Not a bit," cried Doyle; "that's just my writing."

"Open it!" cried the others, thronging up to him.

Satherwaite obeyed, wondering. Within the wrappers was a pocket memorandum book, a simple thing of cheap red leather. Some one laughed uncertainly. Satherwaite, very red, ran his finger over the edges of the leaves, examined it long, as though he had never seen anything like it before, and placed it in his waistcoat pocket.

"I—I—" he began.

"Chop it off!" cried some one joyously.

"I'm awfully much obliged to—to whoever—"

"It's from the gang," said Doyle.

"With a Merry Christmas," said Ailworth.

"Thank you—gang," said Satherwaite.

The distribution went on, but presently, when all the rest were crowding about Somers, Satherwaite whipped a package from his pocket and, writing on it hurriedly, was apparently in the act of taking it from the tree, when the others turned again.

"Little Harry Doyle," he read, gravely.

Doyle viewed the package in amazement. He had dressed the tree himself.

"Open it up, old man!"

When he saw the gun-metal paper-knife, he glanced quickly at Satherwaite. He was very red in the face. Satherwaite smiled back, imperturbably. The knife went from hand to hand, awakening enthusiastic admiration.

"But, I say, old man, who gave—?" began Smith.

"I'm awfully much obliged, Satherwaite," said Doyle, "but, really, I couldn't think of taking—"

"Chop it off!" echoed Satherwaite. "Look here, Doyle, it isn't the sort of thing I'd give you from choice; it's a useless sort of toy, but I just happened to have it with me; bought it in the square on the way to give to some one, I didn't know who, and so, if you don't mind, I wish you'd accept it, you know. It'll do to put on the table or—open cans with. If you'd rather not take it, why, chuck it out of the window!"

"It isn't that," cried Doyle; "it's only that it's much too fine—"

"Oh, no, it isn't," said Satherwaite. "Now, then, where's 'Little Alfie Ailworth'?"

Small candy canes followed the packages, and the men drew once more around the hearth, munching the pink and white confectionery, enjoyingly. Smith insisted upon having the cranberries, and wore them around his neck. The pop-corn was distributed equally, and the next day, in the parlor-car, Satherwaite drew his from a pocket together with his handkerchief.

Some one struck up a song, and Doyle remembered that Satherwaite had been in the Glee Club. There was an instant clamor for a song, and Satherwaite, consenting, looked about the room.

"Haven't any thump-box," said Smith. "Can't you go it alone?"

Satherwaite thought he could, and did. He had a rich tenor voice, and he sang all the songs he knew. When it could be done, by hook or by crook, the others joined in the chorus; not too loudly, for it was getting late and proctors have sharp ears. When the last refrain had been repeated for the third time, and silence reigned for the moment, they heard the bell in the near-by tower. They counted its strokes; eight—nine—ten—eleven—twelve.

"Merry Christmas, all!" cried Smith.

In the clamor that ensued, Satherwaite secured his coat and hat. He shook hands all around. Smith insisted upon sharing the cranberries with him, and so looped a string gracefully about his neck. When Satherwaite backed out the door, he still held Doak's pet pipe clenched between his teeth, and Doak, knowing it, said not a word.

"Hope you'll come back and see us," called Doyle.

"That's right, old man, don't forget us!" shouted Ailworth.

And Satherwaite, promising again and again not to, stumbled his way down the dark stairs.

Outside, he glanced gratefully up at the lighted panes. Then he grinned, and, scooping a handful of snow, sent it fairly against the glass. Instantly, the windows banged up, and six heads thrust themselves out.

"Good night! Merry Christmas, old man! Happy New Year!"

Something smashed softly against Satherwaite's cheek. He looked back. They were gathering snow from the ledges and throwing snow-balls after him.

"Good shot!" he called. "Merry Christmas!"

The sound of their cries and laughter followed him far down the avenue.

POEMS

Henry Wadsworth Longfellow

· · · · · · · · · · ·

1807–1882

CHRISTMAS BELLS

I heard the bells on Christmas Day
Their old, familiar carols play,
    And wild and sweet
    The words repeat
Of peace on earth, good-will to men!

And thought how, as the day had come,
The belfries of all Christendom
    Had rolled along
    The unbroken song
Of peace on earth, good-will to men!

Till ringing, singing on its way,
The world revolved from night to day,

HENRY WADSWORTH LONGFELLOW

A voice, a chime,
A chant sublime
Of peace on earth, good-will to men!

Then from each black, accursed mouth
The cannon thundered in the South,
And with the sound
The carols drowned
Of peace on earth, good-will to men!

It was as if an earthquake rent
The hearth-stones of a continent,
And made forlorn
The households born
Of peace on earth, good-will to men!

And in despair I bowed my head;
"There is no peace on earth," I said;
"For hate is strong,
And mocks the song
Of peace on earth, good-will to men!"

Then pealed the bells more loud and deep:
"God is not dead, nor doth He sleep;
> The Wrong shall fail,
> The Right prevail,
With peace on earth, good-will to men."

Eliza Cook

1818–1889

CHRISTMAS TIDE

When the merry spring time weaves
    Its peeping bloom and dewy leaves;
    When the primrose opes its eye,
    And the young moth flutters by;
    When the plaintive turtle dove
    Pours its notes of peace and love;
And the clear sun flings its glory bright and
wide—
    Yet, my soul will own
    More joy in winter's frown,
And wake with warmer flush at Christmas tide.

    The summer beams may shine
    On the rich and curling vine,

And the noon-tide rays light up
The tulip's dazzling cup:
But the pearly misletoe
And the holly-berries' glow
Are not even by the boasted rose outvied;
For the happy hearts beneath
The green and coral wreath
Love the garlands that are twined at Christmas
tide.

Let the autumn days produce
Yellow corn and purple juice,
And Nature's feast be spread
In the fruitage ripe and red;
'Tis grateful to behold
Gushing grapes and fields of gold,
When cheeks are brown'd and red lips deeper
dyed:
But give, oh! give to me
The winter night of glee,
The mirth and plenty seen at Christmas tide.

The northern gust may howl,
The rolling storm-cloud scowl,
King Frost may make a slave
Of the river's rapid wave,
The snow-drift choke the path,
Or the hail-shower spend its wrath;
But the sternest blast right bravely is defied,
While limbs and spirits bound
To the merry minstrel sound,
And social wood-fires blaze at Christmas tide.

The song, the laugh, the shout,
Shall mock the storm without;
And sparkling wine-foam rise
'Neath still more sparkling eyes;
The forms that rarely meet
Then hand to hand shall greet,
And soul pledge soul that leagues too long divide.
Mirth, friendship, love, and light
Shall crown the winter night,
And every glad voice welcome Christmas tide.

But while joy's echo falls
In gay and plenteous halls,
Let the poor and lowly share
The warmth, the sports, the fare;
For the one of humble lot
Must not shiver in his cot,
But claim a bounteous meed from wealth and
pride.
Shed kindly blessings round,
Till no aching heart be found;
And then all hail to merry Christmas tide!

Samuel Taylor Coleridge

1772–1834

A CHRISTMAS CAROL

I.

The Shepherds went their hasty way,
    And found the lowly stable-shed
here the Virgin-Mother lay:
    And now they checked their eager tread,
For to the Babe, that at her bosom clung,
A Mother's song the Virgin-Mother sung.

II.

They told her how a glorious light,
    Streaming from a heavenly throng,

Around them shone, suspending night!
　　While sweeter than a Mother's song,
Blest Angels heralded the Saviour's birth,
Glory to God on high! and Peace on Earth.

III.

She listened to the tale divine,
　　And closer still the Babe she pressed;
And while she cried, the Babe is mine!
　　The milk rushed faster to her breast:
Joy rose within her, like a summer's morn;
Peace, Peace on Earth! the Prince of Peace is
born.

IV.

Thou Mother of the Prince of Peace,
　　Poor, simple, and of low estate!
That Strife should vanish, Battle cease,
　　O why should this thy soul elate?

Sweet Music's loudest note, the Poet's story,—
Did'st thou ne'er love to hear of Fame and Glory?

V.

And is not War a youthful King,
        A stately Hero clad in Mail?
Beneath his footsteps laurels spring;
            Him Earth's majestic monarchs hail
Their Friend, their Playmate! and his bold bright
eye
Compels the maiden's love-confessing sigh.

VI.

"Tell this in some more courtly scene,
        "To maids and youths in robes of state!
"I am a woman poor and mean,
        "And therefore is my Soul elate.
"War is a ruffian, all with guilt defiled,
"That from the aged Father tears his Child!

VII.

"A murderous fiend, by fiends adored,
    "He kills the Sire and starves the Son;
"The Husband kills, and from her board
    "Steals all his Widow's toil had won;
"Plunders God's world of beauty; rends away
"All safety from the Night, all comfort from the
Day.

VIII.

"Then wisely is my soul elate,
    "That Strife should vanish, Battle cease:
"I'm poor and of a low estate,
    "The Mother of the Prince of Peace.
"Joy rises in me, like a summer's morn:
"Peace, Peace on Earth, the Prince of Peace is
born."

Anne Brontë

• • • • • • • • • • •

1820–1849

✧ ✧ ✧ ✧

MUSIC ON CHRISTMAS MORNING

Music I love—but never strain
Could kindle raptures so divine,
So grief assuage, so conquer pain,
And rouse this pensive heart of mine—
As that we hear on Christmas morn
Upon the wintry breezes borne.

Though Darkness still her empire keep,
And hours must pass, ere morning break;
From troubled dreams, or slumbers deep,
That music *kindly* bids us wake:
It calls us, with an angel's voice,
To wake, and worship, and rejoice;

To greet with joy the glorious morn,
Which angels welcomed long ago,
When our redeeming Lord was born,
To bring the light of Heaven below;
The Powers of Darkness to dispel,
And rescue Earth from Death and Hell.

While listening to that sacred strain,
My raptured spirit soars on high;
I seem to hear those songs again
Resounding through the open sky,
That kindled such divine delight,
In those who watched their flocks by night.

With them I celebrate His birth—
Glory to God in highest Heaven,
Good-will to men, and peace on earth,
To us a Saviour-king is given;
Our God is come to claim His own,
And Satan's power is overthrown!

A sinless God, for sinful men,
Descends to suffer and to bleed;
Hell *must* renounce its empire then;
The price is paid, the world is freed,
And Satan's self must now confess
That Christ has earned a *Right* to bless:

Now holy Peace may smile from Heaven,
And heavenly Truth from earth shall spring:
The captive's galling bonds are riven,
For our Redeemer is our king;
And He that gave His blood for men
Will lead us home to God again.

Alfred Lord Tennyson

1809–1892

RING OUT, WILD BELLS

from *In Memoriam*

Ring out, wild bells, to the wild sky,
 The flying cloud, the frosty light:
 The year is dying in the night;
Ring out, wild bells, and let him die.

Ring out the old, ring in the new,
 Ring, happy bells, across the snow:
 The year is going, let him go;
Ring out the false, ring in the true.

Ring out the grief that saps the mind
    For those that here we see no more;
    Ring out the feud of rich and poor,
Ring in redress to all mankind.

Ring out a slowly dying cause,
    And ancient forms of party strife;
    Ring in the nobler modes of life,
With sweeter manners, purer laws.

Ring out the want, the care, the sin,
    The faithless coldness of the times;
    Ring out, ring out my mournful rhymes
But ring the fuller minstrel in.

Ring out false pride in place and blood,
    The civic slander and the spite;
    Ring in the love of truth and right,
Ring in the common love of good.

Ring out old shapes of foul disease;
    Ring out the narrowing lust of gold;
    Ring out the thousand wars of old,
Ring in the thousand years of peace.

Ring in the valiant man and free,
    The larger heart, the kindlier hand;
    Ring out the darkness of the land,
Ring in the Christ that is to be.

William Makepeace Thackeray

1811–1863

THE MAHOGANY TREE

Christmas is here;
Winds whistle shrill,
Icy and chill,
Little care we;
Little we fear
Weather without,
Sheltered about
The Mahogany Tree.

Once on the boughs
Birds of rare plume
Sang, in its bloom.
Night-birds are we;
Here we carouse,

Singing like them,
Perched round the stem
Of the jolly old tree.

Here let us sport,
Boys, as we sit,
Laughter and wit
Flashing so free.
Life is but short—
When we are gone,
Let them sing on,
Round the old tree.

Evenings we knew,
Happy as this;
Faces we miss,
Pleasant to see.
Kind hearts and true,
Gentle and just,
Peace to your dust!
We sing round the tree.

Care, like a dun,
Lurks at the gate:
Let the dog wait;
Happy we'll be!
Drink, every one;
Pile up the coals,
Fill the red bowls,
Round the old tree!

Drain we the cup.—
Friend, art afraid?
Spirits are laid
In the Red Sea.
Mantle it up;
Empty it yet;
Let us forget,
Round the old tree.

Sorrows, begone!
Life and its ills,
Duns and their bills,

Bid we to flee.
Come with the dawn,
Blue-devil sprite!
Leave us to-night,
Round the old tree.

Christina Rossetti

· · · · · · · · · · ·

1830 – 1894

A CHRISTMAS CAROL

In the bleak mid-winter
    Frosty wind made moan,
Earth stood hard as iron,
    Water like a stone;
Snow had fallen, snow on snow,
    Snow on snow,
In the bleak mid-winter
    Long ago.

Our God, Heaven cannot hold Him
    Nor earth sustain;
Heaven and earth shall flee away
    When He comes to reign:

In the bleak midwinter
    A stable-place sufficed
The Lord God Almighty
    Jesus Christ.

Enough for Him, whom cherubim
    Worship night and day,
A breastful of milk
    And a mangerful of hay;
Enough for Him, whom angels
    Fall down before,
The ox and ass and camel
    Which adore.

Angels and archangels
    May have gathered there,
Cherubim and seraphim
    Thronged the air;
But only His mother
    In her maiden bliss
Worshipped the Beloved
    With a kiss.

What can I give Him,
  Poor as I am?
If I were a shepherd
  I would bring a lamb,
If I were a Wise Man
  I would do my part,—
Yet what I can I give Him,
  Give my heart.

Paul Laurence Dunbar

1872–1906

CHRISTMAS IN THE HEART

The snow lies deep upon the ground,
And winter's brightness all around
Decks bravely out the forest sere,
With jewels of the brave old year.
The coasting crowd upon the hill
With some new spirit seems to thrill;
And all the temple bells achime.
Ring out the glee of Christmas time.

In happy homes the brown oak-bough
Vies with the red-gemmed holly now;
And here and there, like pearls, there show
The berries of the mistletoe.
A sprig upon the chandelier

Says to the maidens, "Come not here!"
Even the pauper of the earth
Some kindly gift has cheered to mirth!

Within his chamber, dim and cold,
There sits a grasping miser old.
He has no thought save one of gain,—
To grind and gather and grasp and drain.
A peal of bells, a merry shout
Assail his ear: he gazes out
Upon a world to him all gray,
And snarls, "Why, this is Christmas Day!"

No, man of ice,—for shame, for shame!
For "Christmas Day" is no mere name.
No, not for you this ringing cheer,
This festal season of the year.
And not for you the chime of bells
From holy temple rolls and swells.
In day and deed he has no part—
Who holds not Christmas in his heart!

Robert Bridges

1844–1930

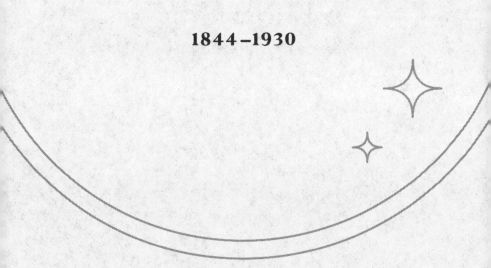

NOEL: CHRISTMAS EVE 1913

A frosty Christmas Eve
    when the stars were shining
Fared I forth alone
    where westward falls the hill,
And from many a village
    in the water'd valley
Distant music reach'd me
    peals of bells aringing:
The constellated sounds
    ran sprinkling on earth's floor
As the dark vault above
    with stars was spangled o'er.

Then sped my thoughts to keep
    that first Christmas of all
When the shepherds watching
    by their folds ere the dawn
Heard music in the fields
    and marveling could not tell
Whether it were angels
    or the bright stars singing.

Now blessed be the tow'rs
    that crown England so fair
That stand up strong in prayer
    unto God for our souls
Blessed be their founders
    (said I) an' our country folk
Who are ringing for Christ
    in the belfries to-night
With arms lifted to clutch
    the rattling ropes that race
Into the dark above
    and the mad romping din.

But to me heard afar
    it was starry music
Angels' song, comforting
    as the comfort of Christ
When he spake tenderly
    to his sorrowful flock:
The old words came to me
    by the riches of time
Mellow'd and transfigured
    as I stood on the hill
Heark'ning in the aspect
    of th' eternal silence.

Joyce Kilmer

. . . .

1886–1918

✧ ✧ ✧ ✧

WARTIME CHRISTMAS

Led by a star, a golden star,
The youngest star, an olden star,
Here the kings and the shepherds are,
Akneeling on the ground.
What did they come to the inn to see?
God in the Highest, and this is He,
A baby asleep on His mother's knee
And with her kisses crowned.

Now is the earth a dreary place,
A troubled place, a weary place.
Peace has hidden her lovely face
And turned in tears away.

Yet the sun, through the war-cloud, sees
Babies asleep on their mother's knees.
While there are love and home—and these—
There shall be Christmas Day.